TIME AND TIME AGAIN

Margaret Judge

Cover design and artwork by Joe Fletcher.

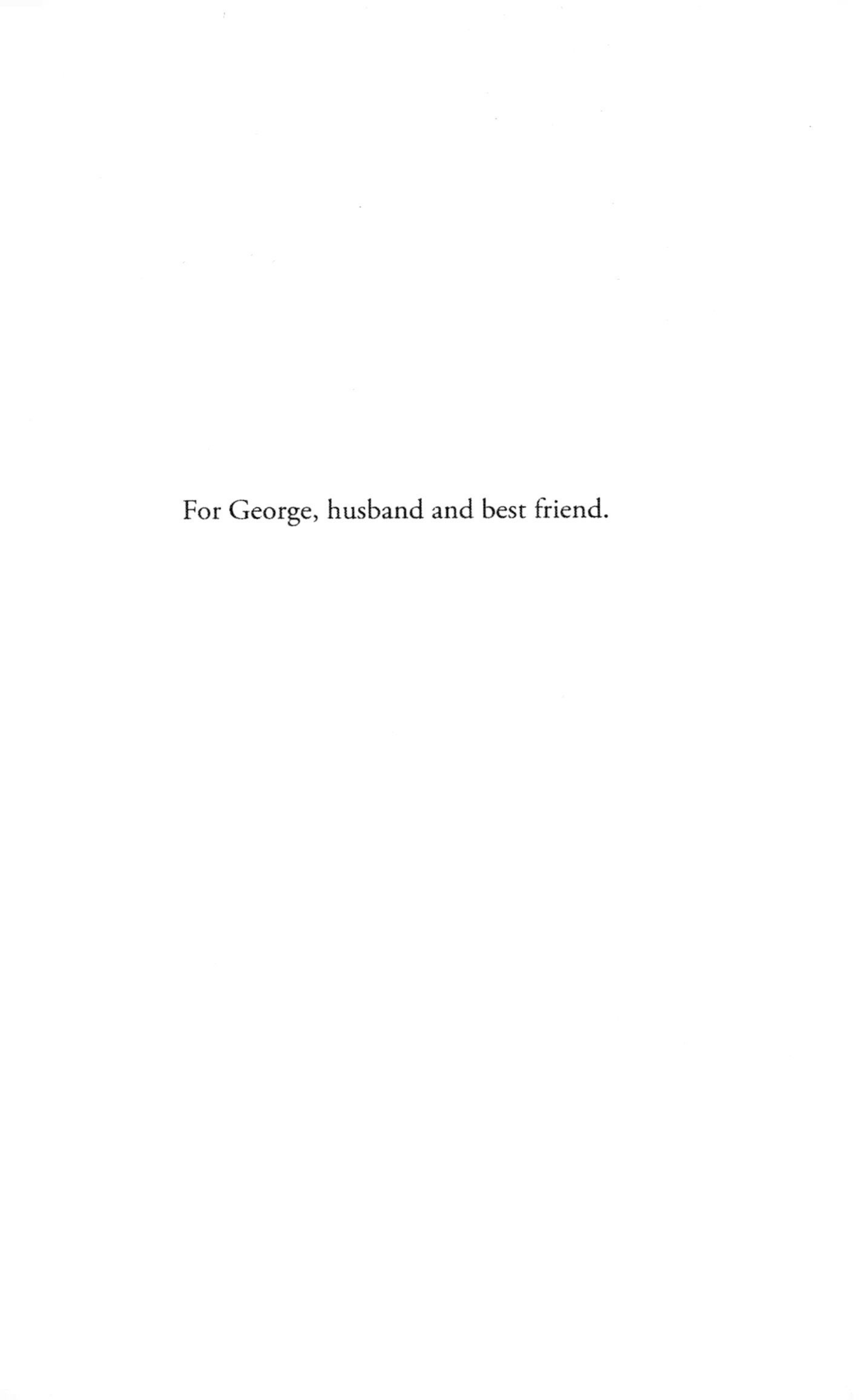

For George, husband and best friend.

Special thanks for help and encouragement
to
George Judge
Jane Stoddard, Lisa Judge
Leigh Robinson, Scott Parris,
Marge Hutchings, Linda Scheffer
and members of the
UC Berkeley Section Writers' Workshop

The ability to control ones' destiny...
comes from constant hard work and courage.

Maya Angelou

Time and Time Again

Prologue

ELLEN ANDREWS
REMEMBERING LILLY PAGE

I knew Lilly Page for only a short time but I've never been able to forget her and often wonder what became of her. It was about 1949 or '50 when her family moved to our small town of Roundhill, Missouri. My husband Tom had finished dental school on the G. I. Bill and bought the Roundhill Dental Practice from Dr. Proctor when he retired. We were living on Charter Street and I was sitting in the big porch swing mending socks one afternoon, when Edwin White came up the front walk. He was a trustee of the Roundhill Bible Church and came to ask if the church could rent Mom's old house to use for a parsonage.

Mom's house stood on Front Street next to the Bible Church and across the street from Collin's Feed Store and the Ready Mix plant. In the past two years a series of deadbeat renters had passed through the house and it had been standing empty since the last renters had moved, leaving three months rent unpaid. I probably should have sold the place when Mom died but I had grown up there and remembered how Mom had scrimped and saved to get the house payments together, and how proud she was the day she walked down to the savings and loan office and made the last payment. Even though the house was rundown, it still seemed like Mom's house and I couldn't bring myself to sell it.

I offered Edwin White a glass of iced tea, and before he left that afternoon we had made a deal for the church to rent the house for their new pastor's family, and I had a crisp yellow check for the first month's rent in my hand.

On the day the new pastor and his family were to move into Mom's house, I peeled apples and baked a pie as a welcoming gift. I put our daughter Trudy into the car and drove down the hill past the cemetery and the Forest Preserve park, turned at the Shell station, and parked in front of the house. I noticed the house needed paint and so did the church next door. A banner with the words VACATION BIBLE SCHOOL hung above the church steps that had been homebase for games of hide-and-seek and red-light-stop when I was growing up.

When I opened the car door I could smell Mom's honeysuckle vine that still climbed a trellis at the end of the porch and couldn't help but wish I could open the door and find Mom in the kitchen.

The old wooden steps creaked as Trudy and I went up to the porch and before I could knock, the new minister met us at the door. He was a slim man who stood ramrod straight, making use of every inch of his height. His dark brown hair was slicked back smoothly and even on the family's moving day he wore a black three piece suit and a necktie. He did not invite us in. Instead, he and the children came out on the porch and his wife stood just inside the screened door, smiling shyly but saying nothing. He shook my hand and introduced himself as Reverend Page, then introduced the children, Lilly and Ralph, but didn't acknowledge that his wife was even there.

Lilly and Ralph, who looked to be about thirteen or fourteen, were attractive children but seemed unusually shy for preacher's kids, who are often cheeky from too much attention from the church ladies. When I asked Lilly what grade she would be in, she looked at her father as if waiting for permission to answer.

"Lilly and Ralph will both be in eighth grade this year," her father said. "Ralph was held back a year." Then he turned to the children and barked orders, "LILLY TAKE THAT PIE TO THE KITCHEN! RALPH, GET MRS. ANDREWS A CHAIR!"

Ralph brought a chair to the porch, then went back inside. After taking the pie into the house, Lilly came back and sat on the porch step beside Trudy. She was a pretty girl with bouncy brown hair, clear blue eyes with dark fringed lashes, and a wide smile. Her mid-calf skirt and brown oxfords, however, made her look different from the teenagers I'd seen in Roundhill. I wondered if she wore those clothes because they were all the family could afford or if her father didn't want her wearing the current style of short skirts.

I sat down on the kitchen chair that Ralph had carried out and Reverend Page remained standing. His movements were sudden and quick, but he spoke slowly and deliberately as if each word he had to say was important. He told me he had been preaching since he was seventeen, when he had received his "call". Then rubbing his hands together, he expounded on how fortunate the Roundhill Bible Church was to have him as a pastor. As we talked I found he had an opinion on every subject and seemed to think his opinions were the only correct ones. I knew the Bible Church was a small, conservative congregation and couldn't help but wonder how they were going to get along with this minister.

While Reverend Page and I talked, Lilly took Trudy's hand and led her into the yard. I could hear Lilly singing "Ring Around the Rosy" and Trudy's laugh as they played. When it was time to go, Trudy was wearing a crown of white clover blossoms that Lilly had made for her.

"I like Lilly," Trudy said when we were in the car.

"Yes, she's nice," I said, and wondered if Lilly might be a good babysitter for Trudy. I needed one every week because my friend Evelyn and I liked to drive into Springfield on Saturday mornings to shop. Evelyn didn't have to worry about a sitter because Lewis could stay with Carrie, but Tom always worked on Saturdays so I had to have someone come to the house to take care of Trudy.

After talking it over with Tom, I decided to ask Lilly to stay with Trudy on Saturday mornings. I thought I should ask her mother before I approached Lilly, so I stopped by the house on a Wednesday afternoon. The Reverend Page was not there and again, I was not invited in.

Mrs. Page stepped out onto the porch, wiping her hands on the apron she wore over her cotton house dress. She stood squinting in the glare of the sun, and I could see that she must have been pretty when she was young and that it was from her that Lilly got her good looks. Time had taken it's toll, however. She was overweight and her faded brown hair and granny-knot made her look old, older than Reverend Page. I couldn't help but think what an unlikely couple the Pages were, him looking like a dandy in his suit, and shiny black shoes and her looking old enough to be his mother.

When I asked Mrs. Page if Lilly could babysit for me she spoke hesitantly, with a voice that seemed too small for a grown woman.

"I don't know if he would want her to do that," she said. "You'll need to ask him."

It was apparent that Mrs. Page was accustomed to letting her husband make decisions. When I talked to Reverend Page later that week, I told him I would need Lilly to babysit for three hours each Saturday and would pay her fifty cents an hour.

"Will your husband be there?" he asked.

"No, Saturday is Tom's busiest day at his dental office."

"It'll be all right for her to babysit on Saturdays, but don't expect her to babysit at night," he said.

Lilly came each Saturday morning and I enjoyed my shopping trips with Evelyn. When I came home Trudy would be napping, and after Lilly helped put the groceries away we'd have lunch together. Lilly liked tuna fish sandwiches, potato chips, and Coke, things her mother didn't serve at home.

I enjoyed talking to Lilly. I could tell she was a bright girl so I was surprised when she told me she didn't like school and didn't get good grades.

"I used to be a teacher," I said. "You could come here after school and I'll help you with the subjects you're having trouble with."

"I couldn't do that. I have to go straight home after school," she said.

"I hope you'll study and learn all you can in school. That can make a difference in the kind of life you'll have. My mother didn't get an education and she had to do housecleaning for other people and take in washings to support us. I know my life is better than hers because I studied hard and got a scholarship for college. You can do that too."

"I won't be able to go to college," she said. "But Father might want my brother to go."

"How do you know you won't be able to go to college?" I asked.

Lilly balled up her napkin and looked down, studying the rumpled napkin in her lap. "I just know..." she said and her voice trailed off.

By the time May came around, Lilly had been babysitting for me for almost a year and I was trying to think of a really nice gift for her eighth grade graduation. After thinking it over I decided to buy her a dress for the graduation ceremony. It would be nice for her to have a pretty new dress like the other girls would be wearing. I talked to Reverend

Page and got permission for a shopping trip to choose the dress. On the Saturday before graduation, I left Trudy with Evelyn and drove to Springfield with Lilly.

The dress shop had a large stock of pastel dresses and we chose several for Lilly to try. While she was in the dressing room, I found a lovely pale blue dotted-Swiss dress that I hadn't noticed before. Without a thought, I took the dress to the dressing room and stepped inside. When I saw Lilly standing in front of the mirror in her bra and panties, my first thought was that she was getting fat...like her mother. Then, a second glance at her rounded stomach and swollen breasts and I knew she wasn't getting fat, she was pregnant.

I handed the blue dress to Lilly and quickly left the dressing room. The shock of Lilly being pregnant made me weak, like somebody had punched me in the stomach. I put out my hand, steadying myself on a clothes rack. How could it have happened? When could it have happened? Her father was so protective of her, even overprotective. I knew he didn't allow her to date and that he expected her to come directly home from school each day. He always knew where she was.

Then standing among the racks of dresses, it came to me. It must be him...her father! I didn't want to believe it but I felt an instinctive certainty that it was him. The longer I thought about it, the more sure I was.

What should I do? What should I say to Lilly?

By the time Lilly finished trying on dresses and came out of the fitting room, I had decided not to say anything. There was no use to embarrass her unless I could offer help. I would wait and talk to Tom. He'd know what to do.

We bought the blue dotted-Swiss dress, a pair of white slippers, Lilly's first pair of nylon stockings, and a garter belt. My hands shook as I counted out the money and it was very quiet in the car as we drove home. I gripped the steering wheel as if it were my only connection with reality and drove straight to Lilly's house and dropped her off without lunch that day.

That night as soon as Trudy was in bed, I said, "Tom, I made an awful discovery today. I found out Lilly is pregnant."

"What do you mean, discovery? Did she tell you or are you guessing?"

"She didn't say anything but there's no doubt about it, and the worst part is that I think her father is responsible. We've got to help her, Tom. What can we do?"

Tom, ever calm and wise said, "Look, we have no facts. It's all just speculation at this point. Of course we'll do whatever we can to help her, but you can't accuse her father of something like that without proof. For now, we'll have to wait and see what happens."

"Well, there's no doubt that she's pregnant and I'm going to talk to her about it when she comes to babysit on Saturday," I said.

Lilly was on my mind all week. On Friday night Tom and I went to the school to attend the eighth grade graduation ceremony. We sat on folding chairs in the gymnasium and watched Lilly walk across the stage and receive her diploma. She smiled when her name was called and in the blue dress, she was the prettiest girl in her class. The soft gathers of the dress hid her figure and I was sure no one else was aware that anything was amiss.

I didn't sleep much that night. I was awake planning what I would say to Lilly the next day when she came to babysit. I was trying to figure out what I could do to help her.

The next morning Lilly didn't come. I called Evelyn and told her to go shopping without me, then put Trudy in the car and drove down the hill. When I got to the Page's house, I could see the truck was not parked in its usual place in the alley beside the house. I left Trudy in the car and walked up the steps onto the porch and looked through the windows. The living room was empty. I opened the door, went inside, and walked from room to room, but there wasn't a trace of the Page family. They had moved in the night.

The townspeople were surprised. The church congregation was shocked, and everyone wondered why the pastor's family would leave town in the dark of night.Tom and I knew why, but we couldn't do a thing about it.

Part One

LILLY
IN HER OWN WORDS

2

We left Roundhill in the dark, Momma and Father in the cab of the truck and Ralph and me in the back with the furniture. We had loaded the truck quickly, leaving only a little space behind the cab for Ralph and me to ride. Ralph curled up in a blanket and went to sleep but I couldn't sleep. I was thinking of the eighth grade graduation ceremony and how, in the blue dress Mrs. Andrews gave me, I'd looked as good as anybody. I thought about the other girls in my class and how they were sleeping in their own beds in their own houses, instead of moving to another town...another house...another school. Tears slid down my cheeks and I wiped them on the hem of my skirt.

Leaving Roundhill was just one in a long line of moves our family has made. We've lived in lots of small towns, some of them too little to be on a map. Father received his "call" when he was just a boy and left school to travel with an evangelist until he was old enough to have a church of his own. He's proud that he is self-taught and his favorite saying is, "The 'call' is more important than book learning".

Because Father didn't go to college he was never ordained in any of the big denominations, so we go wherever he can find a church that needs him. The churches that hire him are small independent ones with names like Miracle Church of the People, Gospel Assembly, and Victory Fellowship Church. We usually move in the spring when many churches change pastors. Moving from church to church is a lot like playing musical chairs and every year we just hope our family will have a place to land.

Each time we move, we think we'll find a church that will be right for us. When we arrive at a new church, the members come by the parsonage to welcome us. They bring vegetables from their gardens and fresh baked bread or pies. Some of the farmers give us honey from their hives, eggs, and slabs of bacon or cured ham. We make good use of the gifts because they are part of Father's pay.

The first few months at a new church are generally good. There are potluck suppers, summer weddings, and Vacation Bible School. Farmers are busy in the fields and the women occupied with gardening, canning, and taking care of the children who are out of school for the summer. The congregations let Father run the church and they don't seem to mind that Momma doesn't teach Sunday School, lead the singing, or attend prayer meetings. But after the harvest, during the long winter months, the members aren't so busy and the grumbling begins. Many people think Momma should do more work in the church, others complain about the sermons being too long or too short, or the hymns being too many or too few. Some members don't like the scriptures Father chooses and others don't like his fire and brimstone style of preaching. Father isn't about to change. "I'm doing the Lord's work as I see it," he'll say. "I guess it's time to move to a church that will appreciate me." At the first sign of spring we pack the truck and move again.

I didn't mind moving when I was a little girl and I liked being a preacher's kid then. On Sundays I'd wear my best clothes and sit in the front pew leaning against Momma's silky flowered dress. I'd look up at Father behind the pulpit in his black suit and necktie, and feel proud that he was the most important person in the church. After the service I'd stand at the back of the church beside him and when the church ladies shook Father's hand, they'd pat my head and tell me I was pretty. Sometimes Father took me with him to call on the sick and the shut-ins and they'd be glad just to see a child.

I thought Father loved me then. He called me "Sissy" and brought me a Tootsie Roll or a lollipop when he came home from the grocery store. In the evenings he sang songs to Ralph and me or told us stories about David and Goliath, Daniel in the lion's den, and Jacob's coat of many colors. I'd sit on his lap leaning against him, his arms holding me close, and I felt special.

On my thirteenth birthday everything changed. We were living in Centerville, Oklahoma. In my mind I can still see the little town of Centerville and the parsonage that was painted green. I remember the storefront church, that had rows of folding chairs instead of pews, and I remember my seventh grade teacher, Mrs. Ray. She invited me to her house once but Father wouldn't let me go. "Nosy teacher," he said. "She just wants to know our business."

It was a sultry day on my birthday. The porch roof gave little protection from the slanting rays of the afternoon sun. Sweat trickled down my neck as Ralph and I sat on the wooden steps playing dominoes. Momma had kicked off her shoes and was sitting in the porch swing with her dress folded up above her knees. She sat motionless, staring at the parched yard that was as brown as a burlap sack.

"It's too hot to play dominoes," Ralph grumbled. "Can we play under the hose?"

"Oh yes, please, Momma, let us cool off!" I chimed in.

"Well, just for a few minutes before he gets home. We can't

waste water, so only for a few minutes, understand?"

Ralph and I ran into the yard, jumping and hopping because the stiff, dry grass pricked the soles of our feet. Momma turned on the hose and we ran back and forth through the water, shrieking as the ice cold spray hit our warm backs and soaked our tee shirts and shorts. Momma sprayed her own feet and then held the hose high, pointing the spray toward the sun.

"A rainbow! A rainbow!" I squealed, "It's for my birthday! It's my special birthday rainbow!"

The spray was pointed up and the water fell down like raindrops. Ralph and I stood under the spray letting the water soak us. We threw our heads back and opened our mouths, trying to catch drops of water to cool our throats.

We laughed when Momma joked, "If you get too wet you'll shrink and then you'll be little kids again!"

Ralph exclaimed, "Lilly's shirt has already shrunk!"

I looked down, embarrassed to see the outline of my two breasts through my wet shirt.

Just then Father came around the corner of the house. When he saw us he started walking fast. His face was red, his eyes were bulging, and his nostrils flared like an angry bull.

"GET YOURSELF INSIDE THE HOUSE, LILLY!" he bellowed.

Turning to Momma, he yelled, "WHAT DO YOU MEAN LETTING HER OUT LIKE THAT?"

Momma ducked her head and said, "Sorry, sorry."

Sorry was a word she used often.

Ralph and I obeyed Father. We scurried into the house to dress. Tears stung my eyes as I pulled a dry shirt over my head. Why did Father pick on me? He hadn't said a cross word to Ralph.

That evening a slight breeze came up and we ate supper on a folding table on the porch. Momma brought out the birthday cake and my present. I couldn't take my eyes off the long flat box and couldn't imagine what my present could be. I knew it would be something Father had chosen because he was the one who did all the shopping for our family. He handled the money and Momma never left home except to go to church.

When I opened the box I found a comb, a brush and a hand mirror: a whole set decorated with little blue flowers. I was pleased with such a grownup gift and ran around the table and kissed Father. He gave me a hug and said, "You're my special girl."

I went to my room and arranged the comb, brush, and mirror on my dresser, then put my nightgown on and crawled between the sheets. I was watching the filmy white curtain change shapes as it billowed in the breeze, when Father came into my room and sat on the side of my bed.

"I've already said my prayers," I said.

Father didn't say anything. He put his finger over his lips to signal me to be quiet as he reached down and unbuttoned my night gown. Then he whispered, "I want to see your rose buds."

I knew what he meant right away and I felt my face go hot. I didn't want him to look at my breasts that had grown big enough to jiggle when I moved. I shook my head from side to side and started squirming, trying to get away. I rolled to the far side of the bed but he flopped down on the bed and grabbed me from behind, cupping my breasts in his big hands. His voice sounded strange as he said, "Stop struggling. I'm not going to hurt you."

He pulled me to him and his face was close to mine. He looked different with his eyes half closed and his mouth open. I could see his pink tongue and could smell coffee on his breath. I tried to get away but he pulled me close, his whiskers chafing my cheek as he rolled over on top of me and pulled my nightgown up. My heart was hammering and I couldn't seem to get my breath.

"No, please, please, no!" I said, before he clamped one

hand over my mouth.

I pushed hard against him but he was strong and all his weight was on me. I couldn't push him away. I squeezed my eyes shut, but hot tears leaked out and rolled down my cheeks. I gasped to keep from screaming with the pain.

When he finally rolled over and got off the bed, he was breathing fast, his face was red, and drops of sweat ran off his forehead. His voice was gruff as he said, "Button up your nightgown and don't say a word about this to anybody."

I waited until he left, closing the door behind him, before letting the sobs take over. I was cold and my body felt as if it didn't belong to me. I pulled my knees to my chest, hugging them, trying to ignore the pain of what felt like an open wound between my legs. I thought about what had happened and ran it through my mind again and again. My own father had used his body to hurt me. How could he do that if he loved me?

It seemed like the worst thing in the world had happened to me. I had been hurt by the person I loved most. My chest felt hollow, like my heart had shrunk and left an empty space inside me. I covered my face with my hands and couldn't stop sobbing.

My stomach lurched and I felt nausea rising in my throat. I clenched my jaws shut to hold back the vomit and pulled the sheet over my head, then wept until there were no tears left in me. Finally, I fell into a fitful sleep filled with dreams of Father's sweating face close to mine, of his hot panting breath against my neck, of his heavy body crushing me.

I awakened with the first streaks of morning light. When I opened my eyes, I thought it must have all been a bad dream, but when I moved I knew it had been very real. I was sore and could hardly walk as I went down the hall to the bathroom. When I crawled back into bed, I noticed brown spots of blood, already dry, on the white sheet.

I heard Father leave the house, then Momma came into my room with a cup of hot cocoa for me. She sat on the side of my bed, her face white and taut as a mask, her lips a tight thin line.

"You're a woman now. It won't hurt as much next time."

"Next time?" I said with a catch in my throat.

"Women have to do things they wish they didn't have to do," she said. "It's part of being a woman."

Was this part of being a woman? Was this part of growing up....like getting your monthly period? Did it happen to other girls? Surely not. No....no! What happened wasn't normal. It was wrong! It was one of those sins Father preached about: fornication or adultery.

"Remember," Momma said. "You mustn't tell anyone or you could get us all in a lot of trouble. Father could lose his job and might not be able to get another one. We wouldn't have money and our family couldn't stay together. Promise me you won't tell."

"I promise," I said.

I wanted to stay hidden in my bedroom when Father came home at noon that day, but Momma told me I must come to the table for lunch.

"Get a bath and you'll feel better," she said. "You know he wants us to have our meals together and we don't want to upset him."

I went to the table. Father said grace as usual, then Momma ladled creamy potato soup into the blue bowls and cut thick slices of bread from the loaf. I watched everybody pick up their spoons and eat as if today's lunch was just like yesterday's.

I stared into my bowl and stirred my soup, not able to look at Father. Then Momma said she was going to make peanut butter cookies that afternoon, and Ralph said he was going to the drainage ditch with Frankie Rooke to pick cat-tails. Finally I caught on, they were pretending nothing had happened. Maybe if we all pretended it hadn't happened, our family wouldn't change.

I picked up my knife and spread butter on my bread. I tried to eat but my heart seemed stuck in my throat and I couldn't swallow. When Momma noticed I wasn't eating, she reached for my bread and ate it.

As soon as Father pushed his chair back from the table, I rushed to the sink and dumped my soup. The milky liquid flowed down the drain, leaving only lumps of potatoes and onions in the garbage strainer in the corner of the sink. As I left the kitchen, I glanced back and saw Momma picking the cold lumps of potatoes from the garbage strainer and eating them. I knew then that she was upset about what had happened, but I also knew she couldn't help me. She was just a helpless woman, and at that moment I felt helpless too.

I tried to push the memory of what had happened with Father out of my mind but the ache in my heart wouldn't go away. I knew I was changed. I felt as if some part of me was missing, like a book with the pages ripped out.

I went to school, but stayed to myself. I felt different from the other girls and was afraid they would find out about me. My grades went down and when my teacher asked me why, I couldn't tell her.

It had been a moonlight night when we loaded the truck and left Roundhill but by the time we crossed the state line, clouds filled the sky. At dawn, Father pulled into a filling station and put gas in the truck.

"Red in the morning...sailors take warning," he said, looking at the red streaked sky. "We better get the tarpaulin on."

Father and Ralph got the tarp over the furniture and tied in place, then Father went across the road and brought back a sack of donuts. Their greasy, sweet smell sickened me and I ran to a ditch to vomit.

Momma gave me a handful of soda crackers and said, "She better ride up front with us".

I climbed into the cab and sat on the seat between them. I put my head on Momma's shoulder that was soft as a pillow, and finally slept.

Cracks of thunder and flashes of lightning awakened me. Raindrops drummed on the metal roof of the truck, and ran onto the windshield faster than the wipers could clear them. By the time we turned off the oiled road into Aunt

Callie's lane, rainwater had collected in puddles on top of the tarp that covered the furniture and the rain had turned the narrow lane into mud that was slick as ice. Father down-shifted and turned the wheels sharply, but the truck lurched, skidded, and slipped sideways, settling in the ditch with the two right wheels mired down to the rims in mud.

We climbed out of the truck, and Momma and I made a bee-line toward the house while Father and Ralph stayed to dig the truck out of the mud. For once I felt lucky to be a girl.

The old house stood at the edge of a stand of hickory and walnut trees on a bluff above the river. The flat, corrugated tin roof and weathered, gray siding made it look more like a cabin than a house. An old metal glider with flowered cushions sat on one side of the front door and a washing machine on the other. Two coon dogs, not willing to get wet, yapped at us from the long narrow porch. This was where Momma and I were to stay *until my time came*. No one ever mentioned a baby, it was always *when my time came*.

We brushed water from our jackets and wiped our feet on rag rugs. The door was opened by Callie, Father's youngest sister. Although she was my aunt, I had seen her only once and never been to her house. Her husband had walked out two years before and left her and the little girls on their own. People couldn't understand why she stayed in such an isolated place without a man around, but I think she stayed so her husband could find her if he ever came back. She worked at the shoe factory in Baxter and needed a babysitter for the girls. Momma and I would babysit and do housework in exchange for a place to stay until Father came back for us.

The floorboards groaned under our feet when we stepped into the main room that served as a sitting room and kitchen. Callie hugged us, then went to the cast-iron cook-stove to stoke up the fire. Lifting the lid, she put a scoop of corncobs and a stick of wood into the fire box and Momma and I hovered near the warmth. Callie dipped water from a bucket to fill the coffeepot and put it on to perk. After wiping the green and white checkered oil-cloth that covered the table, she set out a sugar bowl and a crock of thick cream.

"Might as well sit awhile," she said. "We'll know it's done when it smells like coffee."

I sat on the couch that was covered with a quilt to protect it, or maybe to hide it...I didn't know which. The wooden floor was scattered with braided rugs and there were crocheted doilies on the backs and arms of the overstuffed chairs. A bowl filled with plastic fruit sat on top of the pie safe and a philodendron plant hung from a hook in the ceiling, its leaves drooping toward the floor. I glanced at the wash stand and basin in the corner near the stove, and asked where the bathroom was.

"It's just out back," Callie said.

Father and Ralph came in to wash up and and have a cup of coffee, then Father said, "Ralph and I better get on our way while we can still make it out the lane."

He and Ralph would move into the parsonage at his new preaching job and batch it until Momma and I could join them.

He pulled a roll of money from his pocket and peeled off three bills and gave them to Callie. "This is to help with groceries and for the midwife when Lilly's *time comes,*" he said.

The next five months seemed like five years to me. I had heard about miscarriages and every day I prayed for one, but my stomach just kept growing. I was ashamed of my bulging belly that made people think I had been a bad girl. Even Callie thought I had gotten into trouble with a boy. "I hope you've learned your lesson and will stay away from boys from now on," she said, as she showed me how to hold a crochet hook and taught me to do the chain stitch.

As my skirts got tighter, Momma cut the waist bands and set in material to expand them. The material didn't match the skirts but it didn't matter, nobody ever saw me. I never left Callie's place and if the meter man or the Omar bread man came up the lane, I had plenty of time to run into the house to hide.

Many afternoons I sat on the porch steps in the sun and cried, sure that my whole life was ruined. I had wanted to be like Mrs. Andrews and finish high school, go to college, and have a nice husband, but I had lost all hope that would happen. I didn't know what would become of me. I felt tired and weak, and so sad I didn't want to do anything, not even wash my hair. I hated my life and wished I could die.

One afternoon I took a long walk and ended up at the river's edge. The water was still and deep, even peaceful. I gathered stones and threw them into the water, little stones at first and then bigger ones. I watched shiny rings spread on the muddy water as each stone sank and disappeared, and wondered if I could sink and disappear so easily.

Holding on to a willow branch, I leaned forward over the water, then a little farther forward until I could see my blurred face and big belly reflected in the river beneath me. I would make a big splash if I were to let go and drop into the water.

"Hey! Whatcha doin?"

Startled and holding tight to the willow branch, I pulled myself upright on the bank and looked behind me. A girl about my age stood beside a sycamore tree.

"I'm Lyla," she said. Her voice was as soft as her skin was pale.

"I'm Lilly," I said, looking into her eyes that matched the color of the violet dress she wore.

"You livin' over at Callie's?"

"Yes," I said.

"I heard you was there."

"I'll just be there till November," I said.

"Who gotcha in trouble?"

I didn't know what to say. I couldn't tell her my own father did it, and when I didn't answer, she said, " Did you like 'it'...doin' 'it'....was it romantic?"

"No, no!" I screamed. "I didn't want to do it and it wasn't my fault!"

She stepped back, her pale face bathed in sunlight, and said, "Sorry, I didn't mean to set you off." Then she turned and walked away.

"It wasn't my fault! It wasn't my fault!" I shouted again and again until she was out of sight.

I was breathing fast and couldn't hold back my tears, but even so, I felt better for having told somebody the real truth...that I really wasn't the one to blame.

I wiped my eyes and nose on my shirttail and sat down in the warm, dry leaves. I picked up a hickory stick and scratched my name in the dust, then leaned back against a stump. I stayed there a long time, hoping Momma and Callie would miss me and come to find me. I listened for the rustle of leaves or the sound of footsteps on the path but nobody came, so when the sun dropped behind the trees, I climbed the hill back to Callie's house.

I never saw Lyla again, but I've thought of her often over the years, wondering if she was really an angel who came to the river to save my life...and Rosie's life too.

The first snow came early in November, and Callie started parking her Ford on the side of the county road and walking in and out of the lane. I heard her say to Momma, "Sure hope we're not having a snowstorm when Lilly's labor begins and I have to fetch the mid-wife."

"It'll likely be at the time of the full moon," Momma said." I swear the full moon always brings on childbirth."

From then on I looked at the moon every night when I went to the outhouse. At first it looked like a big cookie with a bite off of one side, but night by night I could see it was growing just like my belly.

As the moon got fuller, I worried about just what would happen to me *when my time came.* The words *labor* and *childbirth* scared me. I'd overheard some girls at school whisper about how babies were born, but they always changed the subject when I came around. They didn't talk about that stuff with a preacher's kid.

I wanted to talk to somebody about what to expect and decided to ask Callie. It had been only a few years since her girls were born so she should remember what it was like. I waited until Momma and the girls had gone to bed and

Callie was taking a bath. She stood on a green towel, close to the stove, her back turned toward me. I watched her lift her arms and pull her shirt over her head, then reach behind her back to unhook her bra. She washed her upper body and dried it quickly, then slipped her flannel nightgown over her head before she unbuttoned her slacks and let them fall to the floor. She squeezed out the wash rag and reached up under the nightgown and washed her bottom half.

I said, "Callie, tell me what it's like to have a baby."

She finished washing and emptied the basin into the slop jar, then turned to face me. There was a harshness in her voice and she sounded a lot like Father as she said, "You'll find out soon enough. Millions of women have survived it and you'll survive it too."

On November tenth I awakened in the middle of the night with a backache. From my window I could see the moon was high in the night sky, and it was full. A shiver ran through my body and I was shaking with fear. I got out of bed and went to the main room and walked round and round, past the couch to the stove and back again. My back ached and my stomach cramped. When I bumped into the rocking chair, Momma heard me and came out of the bedroom.

"Is it bad?" she asked.

"Not too bad," I whispered, still trying to be quiet so Callie and the girls wouldn't hear me.

Just then a giant cramp clutched me and water gushed down my leg. Momma put a towel between my legs and led me to the bed. I knew *my time had come* and I didn't want to go through with it, but I had no choice.

The next hours seemed to pass in slow motion as the pains grew worse. At dawn Callie came and stood in the doorway of the bedroom.

"It's time to get the midwife," Momma said.

Callie got the girls out of bed and they left the house without breakfast. She took the girls to stay with a friend, then brought the midwife back before she went to work.

Wave after wave of pain racked my body and I bit my knuckles to keep from crying out. I wanted to be brave but grunts and screams that I couldn't hold back spilled out of my mouth.

"Pray, Lilly," Momma said. "Pray."

I prayed, but I didn't expect any help from God. I'd learned that He didn't answer my prayers.

Finally, around dusk that evening, just when I thought I couldn't bear down one more time, the baby finally came out. Momma held it up for me to see. I was limp as a dish rag but I raised myself on one elbow to look. It was a measly little thing, wet and covered with a whitish film. Its eyes were still closed and its tiny puckered face made it look more like a newborn kitten than a real person.

"It's a girl," Momma said. " We'll name her Rosie."

I turned to face the wall.

I stayed in bed for the next week and it was wonderful to be able to sleep on my stomach again. Momma brought my food to the bed and I used the chamber pot so I didn't have to run to the outhouse. Momma bound my breasts tight but sometimes I'd hear the baby's cry coming from the other room and my breasts would fill and ache.

When Momma brought the baby into the bedroom I'd turn my back, not wanting to have anything to do with it.

"Don't you want to see your little sister?" Momma asked, her voice sickening sweet. I could tell she was happy about the baby...as if I'd given her a gift.

When I finally dressed and went out to the main room, I couldn't help but see the baby. She lay in a drawer Momma had taken from the dresser and lined with a quilt. The baby was covered with a pink flannel blanket and all I could see was her little round head and two small hands with tiny fingers. At ten days old, she looked more human than she had when she was born. I looked down at her and her navy blue eyes stared back at me. She looked wise, as if maybe she knew that no matter what Momma said, I was really the one who was her mother.

2

Father and Ralph came to pick us up on Thanksgiving Day and and took us to the new parsonage. The next Sunday, Father announced in church that he and Momma had been blessed with a baby daughter named Rosie. He told the church members that I had rheumatic fever and wasn't well enough to go to school that year.

The new parsonage was in the country but was much nicer than Callie's house. There was a bathroom, an electric stove, and even a telephone so Father's parishioners could call him. There were three bedrooms so Ralph and I each had a room of our own and the baby's crib was set up in Momma and Father's room.

Rosie had been scrawny and bald when she was born but by the time she was six months old she'd changed and was as cute as pie. Her eyes were blue like mine, and silky blond hair covered her head. Her round pink cheeks and pointed little chin reminded me of a flower so I called her Rosie Posy.

I liked to sit with her on a pallet on the floor and watch her kick and roll around. She'd smile and make gurgling baby sounds when I'd take her little hands in mine and play patty-cake or peek-a-boo with her. She'd squeal when I picked her up and when I held her over my shoulder, she'd snuggle her little face into the curve of my neck. I hadn't expected to love the baby but it was impossible not to love her.

Father was serving as minister to two rural congregations. Each Sunday morning he preached at the Emerson church at eight o'clock, then drove across the county line to preach at the Bennett church at eleven. Father insisted that the family attend both services but because I was supposed to be suffering with rheumatic fever, I was left at home.

Every Sunday I'd help dress Rosie in her pink bonnet and booties so the family could take her to church to show her off. As soon as the truck rolled out the lane, I hurried to do whatever chores Momma had left for me, then I'd set my hair in pin curls and take a long, hot bath. With no one to rush me out of the bathroom, I'd stand in front of the mirror and admire my flat stomach. My biggest worry was that I would get pregnant again. I had hoped that after Rosie was born Father would leave me alone, but he came to my room time and time again and I didn't know how to make him stop.

One Sunday Momma told me I should make chili so it would be ready for dinner when the family came home from church. As soon as they left I went to the cellar to get kidney beans and a jar of tomatoes. I climbed down the steep wooden steps, feeling my way along the brick wall. Suddenly, I felt a loose brick shift under my hand and losing my balance, I pitched forward. When I landed on the cellar floor, I was holding the brick in my hand.

Rubbing my scraped knee, I climbed the steps to wedge the brick back in place, but even in the dim light, I could see there was something in the space behind where the brick had been. Reaching into the wall I pulled out a book: *Frenchman's Creek* by Daphne Du Mautier.

Staring at the cover, I wondered when the book had

been put there and whose hands had touched it last. Who would have hidden a book in a parsonage cellar? Could it have been a preacher's daughter like me, hiding her book from a strict father, or maybe a preacher's lonely young wife hiding a book from her husband? I opened the book and found the yellowed pages smelled musty, but the words were clear.

I pressed the brick back in place and took the book to my room and started to read. I was fascinated by the description of the Cornish coast of England and the beautiful Lady Dona. I lost all track of time and was still lying across my bed reading when I heard the back door slam. The family was home and I hadn't even heard the truck come in the lane. I slipped the book under my pillow and ran down the stairs.

Momma looked around the kitchen and said, "Why isn't the dinner ready? What have you been doing, Lilly? It's not like you to forget to do your chores. Hurry down and get the tomatoes and beans so we can get dinner started!"

The winter months were long and gray and I don't know if I would have survived if I hadn't had the book I'd found. I read it over and over and every night before I slept I thought about Dona, who wasn't afraid to stand up to her husband and was strong enough to run away from a life that didn't suit her. Night after night I lay in my bed staring into the darkness, wishing I had black ringlets like Dona, but most of all wishing I could be strong and brave like her. Many afternoons I stood by the window looking at the bare black branches of the maple trees against the gray sky, and thought about running away from Father. I just couldn't figure out how I could do it or where I could go.

Finally, the piles of dirty snow melted and the April rains cleaned and freshened the air. The maple trees set new green buds and the hedge leaves were the size of a squirrel's ear. Tractors ran from early morning to dark, working the ground and planting the crops.

Ralph spaded up the garden and Momma and I planted early lettuce and radishes, then set out a row of onions. I was covering the last of the onion sets when Father came to the garden. His step was quick and there was a smile on his face. A church in Illinois needed an interim pastor and had called to offer him the job.

"It'll be great to be serving only one church again," he said, rubbing his hands together and shifting his weight from one foot to the other in a little dance.

Momma took off her straw hat and picked up the hoe. "I guess the next preacher's family will be eating our lettuce, radishes, and onions," she said.

The next day we packed the truck. Rosie rode in the cab with the folks. Sometimes Momma held her up so she could press her little round nose against the back glass and wave at Ralph and me in the back of the truck, where we rode with the furniture.

Soon after we crossed the Mississippi River into Illinois, we noticed the road getting flatter and straighter and we passed farm after farm with white clapboard houses and red painted barns. Everything seemed neat: square houses, square barns, square corn cribs, and long rows of hedge dividing the farms into square fields. The fence rows were mowed as short as lawns and there was no farm machinery or junk setting around the barnyards.

Dogs barked as our truck rumbled along the oiled roads. We saw women in sun bonnets hoeing in the gardens and tractors, with clouds of dust following them, moving up and down the long fields.

Finally the truck slowed. Ralph got up on his knees and read a sign, LINDEN, POPULATION 2,200. Father turned onto the main street that was just two blocks long. We passed a post office, a bank, and a tiny cafe, then stopped at the lumberyard and asked a man wearing a green John Deere cap, for directions to the Church of the Good Shepherd. He told us that the two big brick churches belonged to the Catholics and the Methodists and the little white church on the west side of town was the one we were looking for.

Father drove to the edge of town and parked the truck in front of the little church, which was a pretty white clapboard building sitting on a square lot of green grass. The slender spire reached above the maple trees toward the fluffy white clouds. Beyond the back fence of the churchyard were coal black fields with small green corn plants marching in perfect rows toward the horizon. The rich black soil and the healthy green plants seemed a promise of something good to come.

The parsonage was a two story house with three bedrooms, a lot like the last one. We unloaded the truck and put up the beds before dark. Momma cooked a pan of corn meal mush for supper and we sprinkled sugar over the hot mush in our bowls, then poured cold milk over it. We ate quickly because we were all exhausted and eager for bedtime.

I climbed the stairs and stretched out in my new bedroom. I had heard that on hot nights in this fertile farmland you could hear the corn grow. I listened but heard nothing.

2

By the time we had been in Linden a couple of months I was beginning to like it. Many mornings I was awakened by the 'pop-pop' of a John Deere tractor in the field behind our house. It was July and the corn leaves were stretching up and the soy bean plants were spreading out. The soy beans needed to be weeded before the plants grew large enough to cover the soil between the rows. Farmers hired crews of teenagers to walk up and down the rows chopping out every visible weed. It was hard work in the summer heat, but a good way to make money for school clothes and I wanted to do it. Ralph was hired right away but I had to ask Father, and he said, "A bean field with a bunch of boys is no place for a girl".

Each morning, still in my nightgown, I padded down the length of the upstairs hall. From the front window I could see the truck, loaded with kids, come to take Ralph to the bean fields. I wished I could go. I felt left out and lonely because I hadn't met anybody my own age in Linden. I wondered if Father would let me start high school in September if he wouldn't even allow me to work in the fields where there were boys. I decided not to beg, but to do everything I could to get on his good side.

I helped Momma clean the house and worked in the garden. Many mornings I went to the garden, looking under the vines for plump round tomatoes and searching through the broad flat leaves of the cucumber plants for shiny green cucumbers. I pulled onions and cut bunches of fragrant dill and carried them to the kitchen. While I washed tomatoes, Momma sterilized the Mason jars and lids. The steamy kitchen filled with a pungent smell as Momma peeled and quartered tomatoes and I filled the sparkling glass jars. She put a rubber ring around the neck of every jar, then screwed the lids on tight to seal them. We carefully placed the filled jars into water that was already boiling in the wash boiler on the stove. We kept the stove going, even on hot days, until the tomatoes were processed and ready to store for the winter.

I sliced and cooked cucumbers while Momma heated a mixture of vinegar, mustard, turmeric, celery seed, sugar and salt. After I packed thin slices of cucumbers, onions and green peppers into jars, Momma transformed them into Bread and Butter Pickles by pouring the hot vinegar mixture over them. When the jars were sealed and cooled, I carried the the jars of green pickles to the cellar and put them on the shelf next to the jars of red tomatoes.

One Saturday, Momma took the yeast, flour, and salt from the cabinet, ready to make bread. After mixing the yeast with warm water, she measured out the flour and found there wasn't enough. Father was still working on his sermon, so he counted out some change and sent me to the store to buy flour.

I headed for the store nearest our house. The owner's name was Henry Baldini and everyone called him Baldy, even though he had a full head of bushy white hair. Baldy's store was set up in the two front rooms of his house, which was located on a large lot that backed up to Gordon's Garage.

When I walked into the store, a bell on the door jingled. Baldy, wearing a white apron, came from the back rooms.

"What can I get for you, young lady?" he asked.

"Five pounds of flour, please."

I watched him scoop flour from the bin, weigh it, and tie the sack with twine.

As he handed the package to me, he said, "Are you the new minister's daughter?"

"Yes, I'm Lilly Page. My father is the pastor at The Church of The Good Shepherd."

"You look like a strong girl. Would you be interested in a job doing housework for my wife and me?"

I was so surprised that I stammered as I said, " I...I'd like that, but I'll have to ask my father".

"Tell your folks that we really need somebody to work for us, and if it's okay with them, just come here on Monday morning."

I had no idea what Father's reaction would be but I rushed home filled with excitement. Maybe I would have a job! Maybe Baldy would let me work in the store. I imagined myself wearing a long white apron, tearing wrapping paper off the big roll, tying packages with twine, and ringing up sales on the big brass cash register.

When I told Father about the job offer, he said he had to think about it and it wasn't until after church on Sunday that he decided I should take the job. I could hardly wait to start!

When I got to Baldy's on Monday, he led me behind the counter and through the door into the back of the house. Even without the two front rooms Baldy used for a store, the house was big and the rooms were filled with heavy furniture and dark rugs. There was a musty smell and I could see dust particles floating in the rays of sunlight that came from the tall windows. They did really need me.

Baldy explained that he would take care of the store

and my job was to clean the house and do laundry every day, then we went into the living room to meet Mrs. Baldini. I was shocked to see she was an invalid. Rheumatism had made her joints stiff and she sat, still as a statue, in a chair that had rollers attached to the legs so she could be scooted from place to place. Her yellowish skin was stretched tight over her bony frame and long gray hair hung limp around her gaunt face. The only thing about her that looked alive were her over-sized gray eyes.

I couldn't imagine what life would be like for someone who couldn't walk, and felt sorry for her.

I reached out to her and touched a bony hand that rested in her lap, "I'm Lilly," I said.

"Call me Florence," she croaked. Even her voice was affected by her disease.

Each morning when I went to work, Baldy would have Florence up and sitting in her chair. After I put the wash water on to heat, I'd brush and braid her hair, some days pinning in a pansy or a daisy that I'd picked on my way to work. While I brushed and braided her hair she talked about growing up in the very house where she still lived. Her father had built the house before the Great Depression and he had owned the first motor car in Linden. She never tired of talking about the olden days when her family was rich and she was healthy.

When I finished braiding her hair I'd tell her she looked pretty...it was only a little lie...then I'd put fresh sheets on her bed and Baldy would help her back to bed. I wondered what she thought about as she lay in bed all day and I figured she must be bored. One day I took the book I'd found and read to her. She liked to listen to the adventure of Lady Dona's romance with the handsome Frenchman and would beg, like a child, for me to read just one more page.

When I had finished reading my book to her, she told me there were books in the attic that had belonged to her mother who'd been a student at Monmouth college. I climbed the narrow wooden stairs and found a room filled with furniture, trunks, boxes, even old toys. The family must have kept everything. I searched through box after box of books, looking for some without too many big words and finally chose three small books bound in red: *Emma, North Hampton,* and *Pride and Prejudice*; all written by the same woman.

I did laundry every day, but I didn't mind because they had an electric washing machine with a wringer attached and they used Oxydol soap instead of the strong smelling, homemade lye soap Momma used.

Hanging the clothes on the line was my favorite job. I carried the wicker laundry basket of clean, wet clothes to the backyard and piece by piece, stretched them along the clothes line, fastening them with wooden clothes pins. I liked the fresh air and the warmth of the sun on my back.

It was while I was hanging clothes one morning that I heard a long, low wolf whistle. I was sure it couldn't be meant for me but I turned around to see where the whistle came from. To my surprise, I saw a very good looking head with black curly hair sticking out from under a car parked in front of Gordon's Garage. In less than a minute, a young guy scooted out from under the car he was repairing and came to the fence.

"Hey, where did you come from?" he asked.

We both had big grins on our faces and I said, "I'm Lilly Page, I work for Baldy."

He stood a head taller than me and when he smiled down at me, a sweet warmth spread through me. He was so cute with his dark snapping eyes and arched eyebrows. His tight knit shirt was stretched over his muscular build and part of a tattoo was visible below one short sleeve. The tattoo made me wonder about his age. If he had gotten it while in the military service he would be at least twenty two, which was probably too old for him to be interested in me.

Motioning toward the garage behind him, he said, "I'm a mechanic at Gordon's. My name's Tony Belcanti."

He looked me right in the eyes. The way he stood, his clear voice, and his big smile made him seem very sure of himself, even a little cocky.

I knew I shouldn't be talking to a guy, so I picked up my basket and started toward the back door, saying, "It was nice to meet you."

"See you later, Lilly!" he called after me.

Before I went inside, I glanced over my shoulder and watched him stride across the grass toward the garage. I hoped I would see him again.

That night I stood in front of the mirror looking at myself for a long time. I wanted to look as beautiful as the models I had seen in Mrs. Andrews' magazines, and I wanted Tony Belcanti to think I was glamourous. Father wouldn't let me wear makeup. Maybe bangs would help; they were popular because Mamie Eisenhower wore her hair with bangs. I found the scissors and it only took a few minutes to cut straight bangs across my forehead. I looked in the mirror, turning to the right side, then to the left. Not bad, I thought. I put the scissors away and went to my room, taking the steps two at a time.

The next time I went to the clothesline, Tony came to the fence and we talked. Then every morning he watched for me and we talked and kidded around while I hung clothes and he drank a mug of coffee. After a couple of weeks I knew a lot about him. He had quit high school to enlist in the Army and that's where he learned to be a mechanic. He liked his job because finding what's wrong with a motor was like solving a puzzle to him. He was fascinated with cars and had a red Chevy that was his pride and joy. His favorite sport was baseball and Joe Dimaggio was his hero.

One day he brought cookies his mother had made. They were called biscotti and were different from any cookies I had tasted. I ate them all myself because I didn't want to take them home. I didn't want my family to know about Tony. He was my secret.

In August the corn stalks dried and lost their green color and the soybean leaves turned yellow and dropped to the ground, exposing the dried pods bulging with beans. Summer was ending and I still didn't know if I'd be going to school that year. On my sixteenth birthday, I blew out my candles and made a wish that Father would let me go to a high school.

On the Friday before school started I came home from Baldy's and gave my wages to Father. As he folded the bills and put them into his pocket, he said, "You've got a good job there with Baldy. There's no use for you to give it up to go to school."

I knew I had to obey Father and I wasn't as disappointed as I'd expected to be. The fall days were warm and sunny and I was glad I didn't have to sit in a classroom. I liked helping Florence and I didn't want to miss seeing Tony every day. I liked having time to play with Rosie, who was funny and cute. I'd take her on walks and she'd chase squirrels and make them scamper across the grass and up the oak trees. She'd giggle when she touched the soft brown woolly worms that crawled along the warm ground. The woolly worms were thick and furry, a sure sign of a cold winter ahead.

I saw Tony every day when I hung the clothes on the line. One morning after hanging the clothes, I climbed over the fence to have a closer look at his car. He had just washed and polished it. The red paint glistened and the chrome sparkled.

"How do you like my car?" he asked.

"It's a beauty," I replied. "It's my favorite color."

"Let me start her up so you can hear the engine purr," he said as he slid into the seat and turned on the key. "I've got her tuned just right. She gets twenty miles to the gallon!"

I looked inside at the leather seats and the shiny dash board with all the little dials. It smelled clean and was very different from Father's old truck.

"Nice, huh? Wanna go for a ride after work?" he asked.

Oh, how I wanted to sit in the seat beside Tony and ride around town with him, but I said, "My father wouldn't allow that."

The next Sunday Tony was in church, sitting down in front where Father couldn't miss him. I looked at the back of his head and the way his hair curled softly behind his ears and wished I'd worn my yellow dress. I could hardly wait for the service to end so I could talk to Tony.

Father read the scripture from Ephesians, about how women must submit to their husbands just as they must submit to the Lord. It was one of Father's favorite texts and I crossed my fingers, hoping he wouldn't preach too long. After half an hour he was still going strong and Rosie squirmed in her seat and Momma started fanning herself, sure signs the sermon was too long. Finally, Father stopped talking and Mrs. Benson struck a cord on the piano. We all stood up and sang "Blessed be the Tie That Binds". Father extended his arms and gave the Benediction, then went to the vestibule to stand and shake hands with the congregation.

I held my breath while I waited for Tony, but he walked right past me without even looking at me. I couldn't understand why he didn't speak to me. Why had he come to our church if he hadn't wanted to see me.

Tony went to the back of the church and shook Father's hand and I heard him say, "Nice sermon, Reverend Page. My name's Tony Belcanti."

"We're glad to have you here. Come again," Father said.

On Monday morning Tony came to the fence with his mug of coffee and the first thing he said was "Hey, I think your dad likes me. We'll let him think we met in church and he'll let you go out with me."

"Maybe," I said.

It made me feel good that Tony wanted me to go out with him, but I wouldn't know how to act on a date. Anyway, I knew Father would never let me go anywhere with a boy, no matter where I had met him.

Tony was in church every Sunday and we pretended we didn't know each other. But we met at the fence between Baldy's store and Gordon's Garage every morning.

As fall turned into winter and the days got colder, I kept hanging clothes outside, insisting it wasn't too cold even when my fingers were almost frozen. Every day, Tony took a break from his work and came to the fence while he had his morning coffee. Sometimes he brought a little treat his mother had made. She never made gingerbread or brownies; it was always biscotti or panettone.

On Valentine's Day, Tony had a package for me. I could feel my face flush and my heart pound as I opened the small red box. Inside was a chain with a little heart on it. No one had ever given me such a beautiful gift.

"Wow! It's beautiful," I said.

Tony laughed softly when he saw how surprised and pleased I was.

"I can't keep this," I said.

He took my hand in his and closed my fingers around the necklace, "I want you to have it even if you can't wear it. Keep it, just don't let your family see it."

Then Tony leaned over the fence and touched his lips to mine. I just stood there hoping he couldn't tell how fast my heart was beating. I liked Tony's soft kiss that was very different from Father's kisses. Tony seemed gentle and I couldn't imagine that he would ever hurt me.

I looked at the delicate gold heart again and I couldn't take my eyes off of it. It was my first piece of jewelry and I wanted to keep it. I thanked Tony and took it home and hid it in the toe of a sock in the back of my dresser drawer.

8

After several big snowstorms in March, the weather turned mild. In late April tractors, with discs and plows attached, crawled out of every machine shed like bears lumbering out of hibernation. The fields were being prepared and the new crop was being planted.

Each morning, I looked out my bedroom window at the fields, watching for the first small plants to appear. In mid-May I saw tiny corn plants stretched across the field, making long green stripes against the black soil. Seeing the new crop reminded me that we had been living in Linden for almost a year. Our family seldom stayed in one place for more than a year, so I shouldn't have been surprised when I heard Father tell Momma it was time to pack up.

I panicked! I couldn't leave without talking to Tony. I couldn't leave without seeing him again.

"I'll go to Baldy's and pick up my wages," I said to Father.

"Okay. You've earned the money so we might as well have it, but hurry."

I ran to Baldy's. He paid me and told me they were sorry to have me leave. Then I hurried to Tony's house. I had never been there and didn't know what to say when his mother came to the door. Before I said a word, Tony stepped out onto the porch and his mother went back inside.

"We're leaving," I said. " I've come to say good-bye."

"What do you mean...leavin'?"

"We're moving. My family is packing up right now."

"YOUR OLD MAN AIN'T TAKIN' YOU NO PLACE!" he shouted. "YOU'RE STAYIN' RIGHT HERE."

"Do you mean you want me to stay? Do you really want me to stay in Linden with you?"

"You're my girl and you're stayin'! Let's go tell him right now! If he gives us any trouble, I'll take him on."

"No, no! I don't want trouble," I said.

I was thrilled that Tony wanted me to stay. Maybe he could help me get away from Father just as the Frenchman had helped Dona run away.

I thought a minute, then said, "Let me take my wages to him and help them pack. They won't know I'm not going with them until they're ready to leave town. I'll slip away just before they go."

"Look, I'm not afraid of him but if that's how you want to do it, we'll do it your way," Tony agreed. "You meet me in front of Gordon's Garage at nine o'clock."

As I turned to go, Tony called after me, "BE THERE AT NINE O'CLOCK!"

When I returned to the house, I gave the money to Father then started taking clothes from the closets and putting them into boxes. When I folded Rosie's little dresses, I couldn't keep the tears back. I wasn't sure I could part with my family, especially Rosie, but then I thought about how much I wanted to get away from Father. I couldn't stand for things to go on as they had been. I hated what he did to me and I hated him. I could hardly stand to look at his face.

I packed my clothes in two brown paper bags. As Father and Ralph started loading the truck, I took the bags and slipped out the back door, then ran the three blocks to Gordon's Garage. Tony wasn't there. The thought crossed my mind that he might not come and I wondered what I would do if he didn't show up. I was out of breath from running and my throat was dry. My chest felt tight and my legs were trembling as I huddled against the dark garage. I looked over toward the back of Baldy's house and saw a light in their kitchen. Maybe they would help me if Tony didn't come.

Finally, I heard the sound of a car. It was Tony's Chevy! He jumped out of the car and unlocked the garage door and drove in. I ran into the garage behind him and he closed the heavy door and locked it. We were hidden inside.

There was a smell of oil and grease in the garage and the battery chargers gave off an eerie green light. It all seemed strange and unreal to me. We crouched down below the windows like children playing hide and seek. Tony peeked out and saw Father's truck drive up and down the street, up and down again and again.

I was nervous and afraid, and could only imagine how furious Father would be if he found us. Suddenly, I heard a loud thr-ump-ump-ump! I screamed and leaped back, thinking Father had come to get me but Tony laughed because it was only the noise of the air compressor kicking on.

"We'll have to wait here until it's safe to leave," he said as he led me to a stack of tires where we could sit down. He sat close to me and leaned toward me and pressed his face into my hair, then with his hand on my chin, turned my face toward his and kissed me.

"Please, not now," I said, pushing him away.

I was grateful to Tony for helping me escape, but I couldn't get my mind off my family, I wondered when they had first missed me. I was sure Father was angry and I imagined Momma was bewildered. Ralph should know why I'd left, but what would little Rosie think when she noticed I wasn't there? Would I ever see any of them again?

I put my hands over my face and cried.

"I thought you'd be happy," Tony said, as he unfolded his big red hanky and handed it to me.

I couldn't speak. I was confused and didn't know if I was happy or sad. I had dreamed of the moment I would get away from Father but I hadn't been sure it would ever happen. Now that it had happened, I was afraid.

Tony put his arm around my shoulders and said, "I'll be takin' care of you from now on."

I began to feel safe with Tony and I leaned against him. We sat there a long time watching car lights splash through the garage windows and listening to the sound of traffic on the street. After several hours the street went quiet. We figured Father had left town and it was safe to leave the garage.

Tony put my bags in his Chevy and I got into the front seat. He opened the garage door, drove outside, then went back to lock up the garage. Back in the car, he gunned the motor and the car shot forward, tires screeching. Tony looked at me out of the corner of his eye and grinned. The car was warm and felt safe. I sat close to Tony and began to feel better, as if I was getting a fresh start.

Tony drove to his Aunt Cecilia's house. She came to the door in a flannel gown and nightcap, her tiny face crosshatched with wrinkles. She was happy to see Tony even at such a late hour. Tony put my bags in the spare room and Cecilia took sheets and quilts from the closet and made the bed for me. She lived alone and was pleased to have someone in the house with her. She hadn't been in Linden long and still wasn't sure she should be living in a village that built its grain elevator taller than its churches.

"You stay with Aunt Cecilia," Tony explained. "Mama

and her priest wouldn't approve of you stayin' at our house until we're married."

I had to get used to the idea that Tony and I would be married. He never asked me. He just said that was the way it would be. Getting married excited me, but it also scared me. I probably would have married anybody to get away from Father, but I had a big worry that I thought about all the time. I was worried because I had never told Tony about what Father had made me do, and he didn't know Rosie was my child.

I stayed with Cecilia for two weeks until Tony could get time off so we could go to Arkansas, where the laws allowed girls my age to marry. As the wedding night drew closer, I became more and more nervous and scared. Thoughts rushed through my mind. Would Tony be able to tell that I wasn't a virgin? Should I tell him about Father? If I didn't tell him the truth before we married, could he divorce me? What would I do if Tony didn't want me? Where could I go?

7

On Saturday, June 1, Tony and I drove to Pine Bluff, Arkansas. We cruised the streets until we found a little white house with a cardboard sign in the window that said, JUSTICE OF THE PEACE. I stayed in the car while Tony went to the door.

"It's all set," he said when he came back to the car. "The justice of the peace will be home at five o'clock. We'll come back then and he'll marry us. His wife and a neighbor lady will be witnesses."

We drove to the edge of town to the Shady Rest Tourist Court. The tall jack pine trees dwarfed the row of identical log cabins with peaked roofs, making them look like game pieces lined up on a Monopoly Board.

Tony went to the office to register, then unlocked the door to one of the cabins. When the door swung open we could see the walls and ceiling of the room were covered with knotty pine paneling. The linoleum was worn and the smell of disinfectant hung heavy in the air. I left the door stand open and pushed the drapes back to let some fresh air and light in the small, dark room.

We washed up and I put on my my blue dotted-Swiss

dress and white slippers. I was thinking about the brides I had seen in Father's churches and wished I could have a white dress with a veil and walk down the aisle of a church to meet Tony at the alter.

"Hurry, Lilly. We don't want to be late." Tony said.

"Help me fasten this," I said, as I held up the heart necklace Tony had given me for Valentines Day.

Tony fastened the chain then kissed the back of my neck. My heart jumped!

We went back to the little white house in town. The justice of the peace asked us to stand in front of the fireplace and his wife gave me a pink rose from her garden.

The justice of the peace asked, "Is there a ring?"

Tony's face crumpled and turned red as he said, "I forgot all about a ring."

"That's okay," the justice of the peace said, "It's not required."

We were married. Tony paid two dollars and the justice of the peace handed the marriage license to him.

Tony grinned and said, "We'll frame this and hang it in our bedroom."

We thanked everyone for the wedding then went to a roadhouse for supper. I couldn't eat one bite but Tony ate his sandwich, every French fry on his plate, and drank two beers. He teased me about being a nervous bride.

When we got back to the cabin, I put my blue dress on a hanger. As I hung it in the tiny closet, I wondered what Mrs. Andrews would think if she knew I had used the eighth grade graduation dress for a wedding dress.

I turned to look at Tony and saw he was watching me. He had his shirt off and at that moment he let his pants drop to the floor, then gave them a kick, leaving them in a pile where they landed. I had admired Tony's good build from the first time I had seen him but I wasn't prepared for the way I felt when I saw him standing nude before me. As

I looked at his smooth skin and his well defined muscles, I thought of the Bible verse about how Man is created in the image of God.

Tony came across the room to me and we kissed, leaning against the closet door. I buried my face in his neck, unable to speak. I felt warm and I wanted Tony to hold me and kiss me. I wanted this to be a special time, but the minute Tony pushed me back onto the bed, in my mind his hot breath against my neck became my father's breath, his big hands became my father's hands, and his movements became my father's movements. My body stiffened and I squeezed my eyes shut tight to block out all thought and feeling of what was happening to me.

When it was over, Tony rolled over and promptly went to sleep. I lay still under the sheet, trying to hold back the tears. I was filled with disappointment. I had thought, because Tony and I were married, our sex would be different. I had wanted our love making to be good, like a real husband and wife, but it had been spoiled because of what Father had done to me. A wave of hatred toward my father washed over me again and I knew that what he had done to me would be part of me forever.

Tony stirred, then turned over, facing me. I wondered if he had been able to tell that this wasn't the first time I'd had sex. He rolled toward me and reached for me again, grabbing me roughly, and we had sex a second time. It was then that I realized I didn't have to worry about what Tony thought. He was so turned inward toward his own pleasure that he hadn't been aware of anything that was going on with me.

8

The next morning, when we opened the door, the world seemed bright after the darkness of the cabin. The air smelled of pine and cedar trees and the sun, shinning through the branches, made scattered dots of yellow light on the gravel parking lot. I noticed a clump of purple hyacinths had opened during the night. Maybe that was a good sign, a sign that things would turn out right for Tony and me after all.

"Mrs. Tony Belcanti, Mrs. Tony Belcanti," I said my new name over and over as we drove back to Linden.

Tony laughed and asked, "Do I hafta call you Mrs. Belcanti instead of Lilly?"

"'Honey will do," I said, with a giggle.

As I look back, I know that riding home in the car that morning was one of the happiest times we had together. We sang "Row, Row, Row Your Boat", "Dixie", and "On Top Of Old Smoky." I was surprised that Tony knew most of the songs Father had taught me. We sang "Tell Me Why" with our voices in perfect harmony, then Tony sang "Five Foot Two, Eyes of Blue." He said that song must have been written about me and I moved closer and pressed my leg against his.

At lunch time we stopped for a sandwich at Stucky's and sat side by side in a booth. Tony told the waitress that we were newlyweds and she gave us a piece of chocolate cake with a candle on it.

Later, when we were back in the car, Tony reached inside his shirt, pulled out a little brown stuffed bear, and gave it to me. It was soft and fuzzy and had a pink ribbon around its neck with a heart on it that said, "Honey Bear."

Surprised, I asked, "When did you buy this?"

"I didn't buy it. I snitched it, just for you."

"Ton-yee," I gasped. "That's stealing. We've got to take it back!"

"They'll never miss it. They've got a whole rack of 'em," he said as he double-clutched the Chevy and peeled out on to the highway.

I felt guilty, as if I had been the one who stole the bear. There was a knot in my stomach and my eyes burned with tears. I slid across the seat away from Tony, and wished I had gotten to know him better before I married him.

It was dark when we got back to Linden and the lightning bugs were winking and blinking when we got out of the car at Cecilia's house. Tony ran into the yard and caught a lightning bug, tore the yellow bulb from its tail and stuck it on my ring finger. "There, now you have a wedding ring," he said and laughed.

I held my left hand out and looked at my finger with the bit of glowing light stuck on it. I tried to smile, but I felt my lips tremble. I didn't want a lightning bug ring instead of a real wedding band.

We picked up my belongings from Cecilia's house and I was happy to be moving in with Tony and his mother.

Mama Belcanti met us at the door with her arms held open and hugged Tony, then turned to me and said, "Tony will always be my little boy no matter how big he gets."

I put my things in Tony's bedroom then asked his mother if I could help with supper.

"No, no. You sit on the couch with Tony."

There was a wonderful smell coming from the kitchen. Mama Belcanti was cooking corn meal mush and I expected to have mush with milk for supper. Instead, when the mush was cooked, she poured it on to a platter, spread it thin, and ladled spicy tomato sauce over it. They called it polenta.

"This is delicious," I said as I took a second helping.

Mama Belcanti was all smiles and she said, "Oh, just wait until tomorrow night. I'll make a special dinner because Father Joseph is coming to make arrangements for your instruction."

"Instruction?"

"Father Joseph will set a time to instruct you so you can become a member of the Church," she said firmly.

"No, no! I've been baptized in my father's church. I can't join another church. We're Protestant."

"You were Protestant," she said. "Now that you are married to Tony, you must become Catholic!"

Her dark eyes narrowed and frown lines creased her forehead. She stared at me, looking straight into my eyes. I had heard of the "evil eye" and it felt like that was what I was getting from my mother-in-law.

I gave Tony a pleading look and I could have jumped up and kissed him when he said, "Lay off, Mama. Give her some time."

Later, when Tony and I were alone in his room, I started to tell him I could never become a Catholic, but he motioned for me to be quiet.

"Don't talk now," he whispered. "These walls are thin as paper and she can hear every word."

Mama Belcanti was a good cook and I seldom saw her without an apron over her black dress. She had been a widow since her husband died in an accident at the grain elevator many years ago, and lived on a pension that came in a brown envelope each month.

At the end of the first week, when Baldy paid me, I folded the bills carefully and put them in my purse. I felt rich because I wouldn't have to give my money to Father. Before I went home I stopped at the drug store and bought a tube of Revlon lipstick. It was a hard choice between "Millionaire Red" and "Poppy Pink" but I chose the "Millionaire Red." Before I paid, I noticed the tiny pots of eye shadow displayed beside the cash register, so I bought some blue eye shadow too.

When I got home, I took my packages to our room and put my makeup away, then put my money in the dresser drawer where it would be safe.

As soon as Tony came in, he asked, "Where's your money?"

When I looked surprised he said, "We have to pay Mama for your room and board. You give your wages to me and I'll pay her."

I gave my money to Tony and he said, "Is this all?"

"I went to Laird's and bought some makeup before I came home."

"Hey, don't do that again. You bring your wages to me. I'm gonna handle the money. You got that?"

I hadn't expected Tony to take my money every week just like Father did, and felt hurt and upset that he didn't trust me to take care of the money I earned. I didn't want to cause trouble so I hid my feelings. Tony and his mother never hid their feelings. In loud voices, they let everybody know when they were upset or angry. I was frightened when they fought and I was devastated when Tony yelled at me.

Tony and I both started work at eight o'clock so we

walked to work together each morning and that was the only time we could talk without Mama Belcanti listening.

One Friday morning as we walked to work, Tony said, "I want to ask a favor. Just for me, please go to church with Mama on Sunday. She has told all her friends about her new daughter-in-law and now she wants to show you off."

I didn't want to go but I would do it for Tony, so I said, "Sure."

On Sunday I put on my favorite yellow dress, my "Millionaire Red" lipstick, and blue eye shadow. I thought I looked great when I looked in the mirror but when I came out of the bedroom, Mama Belcanti gasped.

"This will not do," she said in her harshest voice. "Go wash your face!"

I looked at Tony for support but he just shook his head. I went into the bathroom and washed my face, and it seemed to me that all my hopes of being my own boss were running down the drain with my new makeup. Both Tony and Mama Belcanti wanted to tell me what to do. I had to face the fact that by running away from Father and marrying Tony, I had just traded one boss for two.

8

In July a postcard from my mother came to Baldy's store. I was happy to hear from the family and to have their new address. I didn't mention the card to Tony or his mother. I hid it under the flowered paper that lined the bottom of my dresser drawer.

The very next evening at dinner Mama Belcanti said, "Why would your family leave a nice town like Linden to move to Kentucky where all those hillbillies live?"

Anger welled up inside me. I was furious she had looked in my drawer and found my postcard. I opened my mouth to speak then decided I'd better hold my tongue, so I stared at her, wishing I knew how to give her the "evil eye."

Tony looked up from his spaghetti and said, "I didn't know they had gone to Kentucky. That's good. It means they won't be botherin' us."

Every evening when Tony and I got home from work Mama Belcanti had a big meal ready. She made delicious minestrone soup, pasta, and rich sauces. I liked her food but after a while I started to crave some plain food like my mother cooked. One Friday I bought a dressed chicken from

Baldy and brought it home.

"Since tomorrow is Saturday, I'll cook dinner and let you have a rest," I said to Mama Belcanti. "I'll make a nice dinner for you and Tony. I'll make fried chicken, mashed potatoes, and Jell-o too."

Mama Belcanti looked down her long nose and said, "No, no, no, Tony likes chicken cacciatore and pasta." Then she added, "I'll cook and you can do the dishes."

From then on, I was the dishwasher. That was the only chore she would let me do, yet she constantly complained about all the work she had to do. When I offered to help, she said it was her house so she must take care of it. I still think she did everything for Tony because she wanted him to love her more than he loved me.

I wanted to spend more time with Tony, but he never had time for me. He played baseball on two teams, so between the practices and the games, he wasn't home many evenings and on weekends he met his buddies at the Oaks Tavern.

One Friday night he took me with him to the Oaks. I had never been in a tavern before and held Tony's arm tight as we walked into the dark, smoke-filled room. The tavern was overflowing with people and the jukebox blared country music. I felt like I was walking into a den of iniquity that Father had preached about so often. We sat at a long table with Tony's friends and he ordered a pitcher of beer for him and a bottle of Coke for me. I liked drinking Coke from the frosty, green bottle.

After I finished the Coke, I turned to Tony and whispered, "Where's the toilet?"

"That door right back there." he said. Then in a loud voice he said, "Lilly's going to the ladies' room!"

I felt strange, like everybody was watching, as I walked the length of the tavern and went into the ladies' room door. When I was finished using the toilet and was washing my hands, I noticed a picture of a man, wearing only a fig leaf, hanging near the mirror. He looked something like Adam in the Garden of Eden. The leaf was attached only at the top so I reached out and lifted it. DING-A-LING-DING-A-LING-LING, a loud alarm went off. I felt my face blush and I could hardly breathe as I realized that everybody in the tavern knew I'd peeked. I was so embarrassed I didn't want to leave the ladies' room and when I did, everybody was laughing at me.

Tony was laughing the hardest and he said, "Did you see what you expected?"

I felt so ashamed. I just wanted Tony to take me home. From then on I didn't go to the tavern with Tony. I stayed home, but I didn't like spending the evenings with Mama Belcanti, and most of all, I didn't like Tony coming home late, smelling of beer, and always waking me up to have sex.

8

I was still working at Baldy's and I was disappointed that Tony didn't come to see me on his morning break anymore.

"Tony, I miss you when you don't come out when I'm hanging clothes," I said.

"Hey, now that we're married we see each other every night. We don't need to meet durin' the day," he said.

I felt lonely and began to think of my own family. I missed little Rosie, Momma, and even Ralph. I wondered when I would see them again. I thought about Rosie a lot and wondered if she was safe with Father. She was still just a little girl but it would be only a few years before he might harm her. I knew I had to figure out a way to get her away from Father and wondered if Tony and Mama Belcanti would let Rosie come live with us. I came to the conclusion that it wasn't likely that would ever happen. I would have to find another way to save Rosie.

After thinking about it I decided that if I could make Tony and Mama Belcanti see that I was a good wife, maybe Tony and I could move into a house of our own. Since Mama Belcanti wouldn't let me help her in the house, I planted a vegetable garden. I set out tomatoes for her sauces, and zucchini...Tony liked that.

In September, I ordered tulip bulbs from Burpee's seed catalog and made a flower bed beside the front steps. I had just finished planting the tulip bulbs when I began vomiting every morning. I recognized the symptoms right away and knew I would have a baby in the spring. Tony was thrilled when he learned that we would have a baby. He wanted a son who would be a small replica of him.

It took the tulips that I planted nine months to flower. They were in full bloom...red, yellow, and purple...when Antonio Carlo Belcanti, Jr. was born. Tony's pride at having a son was matched by Mama Belcanti's joy at having a grandson. She took over the care of little Carlo as if he were her own child. She put his crib in her room and insisted on feeding him and bathing him.

"Carlo is every ounce a Belcanti," she said. "He looks exactly like Tony did when he was a baby."

I knew Carlo wasn't every ounce a Belcanti. His blond hair and big round eyes were just like Rosie's. I wanted to take care of little Carlo, to hold him and feed him, but Mama Belcanti said, "You don't know how to take care of a baby. I've had experience. I took care of Tony and you can see how strong and healthy he turned out."

I felt rejected and very sad. I began to think maybe I wasn't good enough to be a mother. Momma had taken Rosie from me and Mama Belcanti was taking little Carlo from me.

When I cried and complained, Tony said, "Hey, you're lucky to have someone to look after the baby. You should get a job."

I decided to take Tony's suggestion and look for a job. Baldy didn't need me because he had hired Polly Ellis while I was pregnant with Carlo. There were not many jobs for women in town, but Kate Austin offered me a job as a waitress in her cafe on Main Street. Tony wouldn't hear of me working in the front of the cafe because he was afraid I might flirt with the men who came there to eat, but he did agree to my taking a job as cook's helper in the kitchen.

I worked along with Kate peeling potatoes, baking pies, and helping dish up the orders. Kate worked fast but took time to teach me how to peel vegetables without wasting any, to make mashed potatoes without lumps, and to roll the pie crusts very thin.

I was glad Father didn't know I was working for Kate Austin because he had often called her a wicked woman. Kate was different from the other women in town and people were suspicious of her because she was a woman without a husband and she had a business of her own. She had gotten a loan and opened the cafe all by herself. Most people predicted she would fail, but she seemed to be making a go of it.

Kate wore bright colors, lots of gold jewelry, and kept her jet black hair pinned up in an untidy knot on top of her head. Some people said she was part gypsy, others hinted that she might be a witch, but I liked Kate. She was a smart lady and always kind to me.

Kate was about fifty, had been married three times, and knew a lot about men. While we worked, we talked and she was like a friend and a mother to me. She was the first person to pay attention when I talked and she realized I had feelings.

One morning as I piled meringue on the lemon pies, I said, "Kate, do you think I should worry about Tony going out every night and leaving me at home with his mother?"

Kate lit the oven then washed her hands and dried them before she came to the worktable and stood across from me. She looked straight into my eyes and said, "You know, Lilly, most men can't be trusted and your Tony is no exception. I wouldn't trust him any farther than I could throw him."

"Well, he is cute and I know girls flirt with him," I

said.

"Listen to me, Girl, Tony has been spoiled by his mama and he's going to take whatever he wants. Women have to look out for themselves. If I were you, I'd hide a few dollars from my pay every week for mad money."

I think she knew I would leave Tony before I knew it.

Kate was a good boss. We were on our feet from seven in the morning until three in the afternoon every day, cooking in the crowded little kitchen where large pots and pans hung over the range and stacks of heavy plates stood ready to be filled.

At noon each weekday the lunch crowd dribbled in. The highway crew was usually first, then the telephone repairmen, the railroad workers, and several long tables of farmers, whose wives didn't want to spend their day cooking and baking for the farm hands. The booth by the front window was always saved for the only two women who ate lunch downtown: Elinor Washburn from the insurance office and Bernice Franklin from the bank.

The menu never changed: ham and beans on Monday, beef and noodles on Tuesday, pork and dressing on Wednesday, meatloaf on Thursday, and fried perch on Friday. Stella, the waitress, took the orders and called them through the little window between the dining room and kitchen. Kate cut and served the meat and I added a scoop of mashed potatoes and a spoonful of canned green beans or peas onto the divided plates.

When the last plate lunch was served, Kate and I sat down together and she'd light a cigarette and reach for her deck of cards. It wasn't an ordinary deck with kings and queens. These cards were larger than playing cards and the backs were decorated with elaborate gold and red scrolls. Each card had a beautiful picture on its face and Kate knew what each card meant. She would do a five-card layout and from the pictures that came up and the position they were in, she could tell how to manage her life. Kate read her cards most days and sometimes other people came to get a reading and they paid Kate for doing it.

I was curious and liked to watch her turn over the cards, which always seemed to come up in different patterns.

One day I asked, "Where did you get those cards?"

"They're very old," she said, "I don't even know where you could get cards like these nowadays. My Czech grandmother brought this deck with her when she came to America. She taught me to read them when I was just a little girl."

"Are they magic?"

"No, Tarot cards aren't magic, but they can make you think about your options and give you some guidance."

She gathered up the cards and said, "Here, shuffle them and let me do a layout for you."

I pulled my hand back as though the cards would burn me. "No, no!"

I didn't want to touch those cards because reading cards seemed like fortune telling and Father had preached that was a sin.

Kate chuckled, tucked a stray curl back into her upswept hair and said, "If you ever want a reading, let me know."

I couldn't help but wonder what the cards might tell me if I let Kate do a reading for me. Then I thought about the part of the Lord's Prayer that says, *Lead me not into temptation, but deliver me from evil.* I knew the cards were tempting me, but could cards made of pasteboard really be evil?

Even though Kate and I worked hard, I was happier in the cafe kitchen than I was at home. Mama Belcanti and I had lots of disagreements. She didn't like sharing her home with me and she tried to keep Carlo and Tony for herself. She wouldn't let me do anything for Tony and she spent all her time with little Carlo, then put him down for a nap so he'd be sleeping when I came home from work. Carlo hardly knew me. She loved it when I tried to pick him up and he would turn away from me and reach his little arms out to her instead.

I had to be at the cafe early every morning to start the pies and Tony didn't go to the garage until eight, so we couldn't walk to work together anymore. We never had a chance to talk without his mother listening and never had a moment alone except in bed.

One Tuesday morning in November, I went to work feeling fine but by ten o'clock my head was hurting.

"I've got a a splitting headache," I told Kate.

"Go on home, Lilly. I don't think we'll be very busy today. I'll manage."

I took my jacket off the hook, picked up my purse, and started for home. When I got to Baldy's, I stopped to buy a box of aspirin. As I left the store and came around the corner, I glanced toward the clothesline. There was Polly Ellis standing by the fence with the laundry basket at her feet, and there was Tony leaning across the fence, holding her hand and looking into her eyes.

My throat tightened and I felt my heart thumping in my chest as I walked toward them. I cleared my throat and when Tony turned around and saw me, his face flushed crimson.

In my calmest voice I said, "I just wanted to let you know I have a headache and Kate let me off."

I turned on my heel and walked home, my head and my heart both throbbing. I went straight into our bedroom and flopped down on the bed. I cried and cried and I didn't even care if Mama Belcanti heard me through the closed door. I stayed in bed all afternoon and didn't get up for supper.

Later, when Tony came to bed, I pretended I was asleep, but I heard him say, "I don't want you followin' me around spyin' on me anymore. If there is one thing I can't stand it's a jealous wife!"

My headache was better the next morning but my heart was still aching. I didn't know what to do about Tony or about his mother and wondered if the Tarot cards could tell me what to do. When I saw Kate I told her I would like to have a reading and that I would pay for it.

"We'll do it right after work today," she said, " but you won't pay me."

I was nervous all day but when the time came, I felt calm as I followed Kate up the stairs to her little apartment over the cafe. We sat at a table and I felt safe sitting across from her.

I didn't know Kate was religious but she reached across the table and took both of my hands in hers and said a prayer, *"May the white light surround us and protect us. May the words we say and the words we hear be acceptable in thy sight. Amen."*

She handed the cards to me and I shuffled them, then gave them back to her. Dealing off of the top of the deck, Kate laid the cards out on the table in the shape of a cross.

She studied the cards and then said, "You have three Major Arcana, suggesting issues of great importance are on your mind. Now is the time to focus on who you are and what you want to be."

Kate continued, "The Nine of Wands indicates the need to transform yourself. This is the time to release the old and look for the new. You can do this because the time is right for change. You are coming into a time of starting anew, a new chapter. You need to spend time alone listening to your inner voice. It knows what is right for you. Follow your inner voice and you'll know what to do and be unafraid."

Kate cocked her head to one side and touched the card at the top of the layout. "It looks like you've suffered a deep tragedy in your life and the single court card, the King of Pentacles, suggests that an older man is involved. You have a fear of authority figures such as teachers, doctors, and ministers and you feel a need to do what they tell you to do. When you blindly obey others, you put them in power over you and things that happen are not all your fault."

She shifted in her chair and said, "Your body card is the Shaman of Swords, which indicates that there are emotions brewing inside that you hesitate to express. You are fearful that someone will get to know you and learn the truth about you. This card shows the need to learn to speak your truth.

This Star card relates to the future. In the upright position it denotes that you will develop skills and special talents that you don't even know you have.

Your Outcome card is the Magician, which indicates that you will be effective in the world. However, the card's position shows there will be an ongoing struggle before this is manifested. But it will come. Your future will be better than your past. There will be success and happiness...maybe a happy marriage later, but much later."

Kate looked up and asked, "Do you want to ask the cards a question?"

I hesitated. I'd never told Kate that Rosie was my child. I took a deep breath and asked, "Will Rosie ever live with me?"

Kate shuffled the cards again and asked me to draw one card. After looking at it, she said, "This card indicates that you are the kind of person who can achieve anything you have a deep passion for. The answer to your question is that if you really want Rosie with you, you will never give up until you achieve that."

"Thank you Kate," I said. "You have really given me some things to think about."

For the next three months I felt blue and down in the dumps. I thought a lot about Tony and about our marriage. I knew I'd failed as a wife and mother and I thought of the Tarot reading and about starting a new chapter in my life. I wondered if I should leave Tony and make a fresh start. Nobody would even care if I left. I knew little Carlo didn't need me because he would be well taken care of by his "nonna", who he preferred to me. I knew Tony would miss me only because he used me for sex, and I was sure Mama Belcanti would be glad to see me gone.

I didn't tell anyone I was leaving. The day I left, I stuffed socks and underwear into a grocery bag and put the money I'd been saving into my purse. I told Kate I needed to pick up my pay and get off a few minutes early that day. She must have guessed that I was leaving on the three o'clock Greyhound, because she wrote good luck on my pay envelope and put an extra ten dollars inside.

My heart was pounding and my mind was racing when I got on the bus and sank into a seat. Here I was, running away from Tony just as I had run away from Father. I wondered if I should go back and try to work things out, but I knew Tony would never change, just as my father would never change. I had come to realize that neither Tony or my father had loved me. Neither had cared about my feelings.

The driver got on the bus and closed the door. As the bus left Linden, I felt a hard, cold lump forming in my throat and I almost choked on my own tears. I was sad and dejected that my marriage to Tony was over and I didn't know when I would see little Carlo again. I knew he wouldn't miss me, but I would miss his sweet baby smell, the feel of his soft skin, and his laugh that sounded like a cackle.

It was still light when I got off the bus at the terminal in Indianapolis. I stood on the concrete boarding area watching the other passengers rush out into the city. I was confused and didn't know which way to turn. Was I the only person who didn't know where I was going? All the way on the bus I had been thinking about what I was leaving behind instead of thinking about what I'd do once I got there.

Checking the line of silver buses parked diagonally along the building, I read the destinations: Chicago, Dayton, Cincinnati, Louisville. I didn't know anybody in any of those places so I decided I might as well stay in Indianapolis.

I went inside the terminal that smelled of hot dogs and scorched coffee. I found the restroom and washed my face, then went into the crowded waiting room and took a seat next to an old woman. I glanced sideways at her wrinkled skin and pearl-colored hair that stuck our from under a green hat. She looked soft and sweet, like somebody's grandmother. I moved closer to her, hoping it would look like we were traveling together.

Each time there was an announcement of a bus leaving, groups of people moved toward the door and soon the crowd in the waiting room had thinned out. When the bus for Dayton was called, the woman beside me stood, picked up her suitcase, and shuffled out the door. We hadn't spoken to each other during the hour or so we had been sitting together, but when she left, I missed having her beside me and felt empty and alone.

I scooted down to the corner of the polished bench and rolled my raincoat into a pillow. I was tired from working all day with Kate and I hadn't slept much the night before. I fell asleep and was dreaming when I felt a tap-tap-tap on the sole of my shoe. My eyes flew open. There was a policeman standing over me.

"This is no hotel, young lady," he said. "You aren't planning on spending the night here are you?"

"Uh, oh no, I didn't mean to fall asleep."

"Are you waiting for somebody?"

"I'm waiting for my aunt. I'm visiting her and she'll be here to pick me up when she gets off work," I said, almost choking on the lie.

"When will that be?"

"I don't know for sure. She may have to work overtime, but I'm supposed to stay right here till she comes for me."

"Well, I'll be around. Let me know if she doesn't show up and I'll help you locate her."

I kept my eye on the policeman as he sauntered the length of the terminal and went outside to the bus bays. As soon as he was out of sight, I put on my raincoat and scurried out the front door.

While I had been in the waiting room, the sun had gone down and the night air was chilly. I pushed my hands deep into my pockets and shivered as I walked close to the buildings, hoping no one would notice me. The street lights were dim and the lamp posts cast long shadows that looked like giant arms stretching across the the street. I wanted to get inside and wondered where I could go.

I walked several blocks before I saw a wedge of greenish light shining on the sidewalk. I made my way toward the light and found it came from the large windows of a storefront. I read the big green neon letters that said LAUNDROLAND LAUNDROMAT.

I pushed the door open to a blast of warm, moist, detergent-scented air. The washing machines were silent but I could hear the huge dryers tossing and jostling clothes, sounding like growling monsters digesting their dinners. Above the noise of the dryers, I could hear the shrill cry of a baby.

I walked toward the back of the room, past a middle-aged man folding jeans and tee shirts. A girl about my age sat in one of the orange plastic chairs holding the crying baby and reading a movie magazine. I sat down and studied the girl. Her limp blond hair hung down across her face, covering one eye. She was wearing a stretched out tee shirt, jeans, and rubber thongs, although it was much too cold for thongs. I started thinking how much better she would look with a good haircut and a little make-up. She could stand to lose five pounds too. That was a habit I had: looking at other people and thinking about how to improve their appearance.

The man finished folding his clothes, put them in a basket, and left. The girl and her baby, who looked to be about Carlo's age, and I were the only people in the laundromat.

Leaning forward out of my orange chair, I cleared my throat and said, "Cute baby."

"Thanks. He's really fussy 'cause he's teethin'."

"I have a baby boy too....but he's with his dad right now."

"You got a picture of him?" she asked.

I took two pictures from my purse and showed her. "This is my baby Carlo, and this is my sister Rosie."

"They look a lot alike, and they both look like you," she said.

A dryer shut off and the girl jumped up and put the magazine on the chair next to me.

"Want to read that?"

"Thanks."

She held the baby on her left hip and took clothes out of the dryer with her right hand, then still holding the baby, tried folding the clothes with one hand. The baby was very unhappy and his cry changed to a scream.

"Could I hold the baby for you while you fold your clothes?"

"He's a mama's boy. He fusses even more if anybody else holds him," she said.

"Okay. You walk with him and calm him down and I'll fold the clothes. I'm Lilly."

"I'm Midge, Midge Helm and this is Rodney."

I folded the diapers, then when a second dryer shut off, I folded the rest of the clothes and stacked them in her basket while she walked up and down the long room, holding the baby over her shoulder. As I folded her husband's BVDs, I was reminded that I had never folded Tony's underwear, that was another one of the things his mother had insisted on doing for him.

"Didn't you bring your own laundry?" Midge asked.

"No, I just came in here to get warm."

"You ain't thinkin' of staying here all night are you?"

"Maybe. I don't have any place to go."

"Whatcha gonna do when they close at 1:00 A.M?" she asked.

"I thought these places would be open all night."

She ran her fingers through her hair, pushing it back so I could see both of her eyes for the first time. "You come on with me. Our place is little but you can sleep on the couch."

"How far is it?" I didn't want to get too far from the bus

terminal in case I decided to catch the bus back to Linden the next day.

"It's just across the parking lot. My husband'll be home after he gets off work at eleven. He's a bus driver."

"Will it be okay with him...for me to spend the night?" I asked.

"I don't know why not."

The baby had finally stopped crying so she put him on top of the clothes in the laundry basket, and we each took a handle and carried it toward a mustard-colored, cement block building at the back of the parking lot. We climbed a metal staircase, then walked single file along a walkway to apartment 203.

I had never been in such a small apartment before and was surprised that anyone could live in such a tiny space. A sagging green couch, a coffee table, and an oak rocking chair filled the little living room. There were stacks of magazines, empty beer cans, and overflowing ashtrays on the coffee table.

"Just put the clothes on the bed," she said as she sat in the rocker, pulled her tee shirt up, and gave her nipple to the eager baby.

I carried the basket to the bedroom and put the clean clothes on the bed, then sat on the couch, watching her nurse her baby. I thought she was lucky to be with her husband and baby and to have a place all their own. I looked around the apartment and thought how she could fix it up. Some cute curtains, a lamp, and pictures on the wall would do wonders.

There was no baby crib so when the baby finally slept, Midge put him on the bed where I had put the clean clothes. I wondered if the baby would sleep in the bed with her and her husband all night.

It was near midnight when her husband came in from

work.

"This is Raymond," Midge said. "And this is Lilly. She needs a place to stay so I told her she could sleep on the couch tonight."

Raymond gave me a smile and said, "Lilly, that's a pretty name. Where'd Midge find you, anyway?"

Before I could answer, Midge said, "She helped me with the clothes at the laundromat because the baby was so fussy."

Midge went into the alcove that was a tiny kitchen and opened a can of tomato soup, added a can of water, and put it on the stove to heat.

"Want some soup?" she asked.

I could see that one can of soup was barely enough for them so I said, "I"ve already had something to eat."

Raymond crushed a handful of soda crackers into his soup, then ate, washing it down with beer. I sat on the couch and leafed through a Silver Screen magazine while they ate. I was thinking how lucky I was to have found them. Maybe I could stay with them until I found a job. I could help with the baby and clean the apartment to repay them. Maybe I could cut Midge's hair for her.

When they finished their soup, Raymond opened a package of Twinkies, threw one to me, and said, "Sweets for the sweet!"

I caught the Twinkie, unwrapped it and squeezed the sweet white filling into my mouth before eating the soft cake. After they finished eating they each smoked a cigarette, then got up, leaving the dishes on the table and the soup pan on the stove.

"Good night." Midge said.

Raymond said,"Night, night. Sleep tight. Don't let the bedbugs bite!"

Even though I knew envy was a sin, I was envious of Midge as I watched her go into the bedroom with her husband and close the door. I wished that Tony loved me and that I was going to bed with him, instead of sleeping on a couch in a strange apartment in a strange city.

I washed the dishes and cleaned up the kitchen before I turned off the light. They didn't have extra pillows or blankets so I put on my raincoat and stretched out on the couch with my arms across my chest and my hands tucked into my armpits. Lying there with the sound of traffic keeping me awake, I wondered why a girl like Midge could make her marriage work and I couldn't. But deep in my heart I knew the answer. It was because of what happened with Father. Nobody was ever going to love a girl like me. A sob caught in my throat, almost choking me and I turned over, pressing my face into the back of the couch to muffle my sobs.

Later, much later, I fell asleep.

Sometime in the night, while it was still very dark, I was awakened by someone getting on the couch with me.

"Tony...Tony, what are you doing here?" I said, my voice soft from sleep.

Then I felt hands touching me...but they were not Tony's hands!

I pushed with all my might. Raymond rolled onto the floor. I jumped up, grabbed my stuff and ran down the stairs, clutching my purse and bag of clothes against my chest and carrying my shoes. I ran, my feet barely touching the cold asphalt as I streaked across the parking lot. I reached the laundromat, grabbed the door handle and pulled with all my might, but the door would not open. It was locked tight. Gasping for breath, I looked behind me but saw no one. I quickly slipped my feet into my shoes and hurried back to the bus terminal.

I was thankful for the warm, lighted terminal but I didn't feel safe there in the middle of the night. I went into the restroom and locked myself in a stall and huddled there, wondering why Raymond had come on to me like that. I was sure I hadn't done anything to lead him on. Could he tell that I was different? Could he guess what Father had done to me?

I thought about Midge and wondered if she had heard the commotion when Raymond fell to the floor and I ran down the stairs. I hoped she wouldn't blame me. She had tried to be my friend.

11

At first light I went to the waiting room and checked the policeman. He was not the same one who had been on duty the night before so I decided it was safe to hang around the terminal for a while. I had coffee and a donut at the lunch counter, then spotted a paperback book someone had left on a bench. It was a mystery by Mickey Spillane. I tried to read but couldn't keep my mind on the story. I had to figure out what I was going to do.

I put my head back and closed my eyes, letting pictures flash through my mind, pictures of me back in Linden with Tony and his mother; then pictures of me with Rosie in a place where I could keep her safe. I knew which picture I wanted. I wanted to find a place where Rosie and I could be together, a place where Father couldn't find us.

As I sat there thinking, I became aware of a young woman sitting across from me. She was dressed in a silky orange blouse and brown suit that must have cost a fortune. Her purse matched her high heeled pumps and I wondered if her toes really came to a point like her shoes did. There was a tan leather suitcase on the floor beside her feet. I looked from her suitcase to my brown paper bag of clothes and wondered what she had done, or not done, to deserve her nice clothes and that beautiful leather suitcase. Was it God's will or was it just luck?

I decided to get out of the bus terminal. I went to the lunch counter and asked the waitress for directions to downtown, then walked several blocks until I saw a bus going east. When I got on and offered the driver a dollar bill he pointed to a sign that said "Exact change only." I thought he would make me get off, but he let me ride until the bus crossed some train tracks and stopped at a big old-fashioned train station. I got off the bus and started walking.

Indianapolis was bigger than I'd expected, a real city with block after block of stores and restaurants. As I walked past a little Italian cafe the smell of tomato sauce and pasta almost pulled me in, but I decided to skip eating and use some of my money to rent a room. I needed some sleep, and a bath too. I walked most of the day and finally found a YWCA on Gulon Road that rented rooms for $2.50 a night. I waited until the sun went down to go inside. The desk clerk looked at my wrinkled raincoat and my paper bag of clothes and frowned, cleared her throat, then finally took my money.

When I had the key in my hand, I went up the steps two at a time. Once inside the little room I leaned back against the door, catching my breath, and feeling thankful to be off the street. I took in the room in a glance. There was a narrow iron bed, a dresser with a small mirror above it, and one straight chair. The wooden floor was bare and the bathroom was down the hall.

As I hung up my raincoat, I noticed the heavy silence in the room and realized I was all alone. All my life I had had somebody with me...somebody to talk to, even to tell me what to do. I walked to the window and looked down on the street that was filled with people, all strangers. What was I doing in a city where I knew no one? I was scared and felt a pressing panic in my chest.

I thought about Tony and Carlo. They were probably having supper right then. I wished I could have some of Mama Belcanti's warm pasta and then sleep in the familiar bed with Tony beside me. Maybe being with Tony wasn't as bad as being alone. Maybe I should have stayed there, that would have been the easiest thing to do. Maybe I should get on the bus in the morning and go back.

Then I thought about how Tony had tricked me into thinking he loved me when he didn't care about me at all. I didn't want to live with a man who treated me like he owned me. I didn't want to be like Momma, always obeying Father and saying, "I'm sorry, I'm sorry," all the time. No! I wouldn't go back to Tony! This was the new beginning the Tarot cards told me about.

I pulled down the window blind, then went to the dresser to look in the mirror. The light was dim and I squinted my eyes, trying to see better. I was shocked to see the waif that stared back at me. My skin looked gray and my eyes were red-rimmed with circles under them. My clothes were rumpled and my hair needed to be washed. I wondered if that unkempt girl I saw in the mirror would be able to find a job. Kate had often told me that a woman must be able to support herself to be free. If I wanted to be free, I would have to find a job fast.

I took the pictures of Carlo and Rosie from my purse and propped them up on the dresser, kicked off my shoes, then went to the bed and sat cross-legged on the flimsy green bedspread. I had to think about what I would do next. I knew the forty-eight dollars in my purse wouldn't last long.

I leaned back on the bed and stretched out, staring at the ceiling, counting the little black holes on the acoustical tile squares. My mind and my body were exhausted and I fell into a deep sleep. I dreamed I was being chased along a dark street and could hear footsteps behind me, getting louder and louder...then suddenly, I sat up startled out of sleep by the sound of real footsteps outside my door. I sat shivering in the dark, listening. Was somebody chasing me? Could it be Father? Tony? Raymond? A stranger off the street below?

I pulled the covers over my head until the noise finally stopped, then still shaking with fear, couldn't get back to sleep. I was thirsty and needed to go to the bathroom, but I was afraid to unlock my door. I didn't have a watch so I had no idea how long it would be until morning but fear kept me locked in the room.

When I finally saw daylight peeking along the edge of the window blind, I opened the door and looked into the hall. It was empty. I dashed to the bathroom and had a shower and washed my hair before anyone else was up.

Back in my room, I stretched out on the bed and decided to rest for just a few minutes. The next thing I knew, I was awakened by sun shining directly in my eyes. I could tell it was close to noon and I was starving. I dressed quickly, went downstairs and walked across the street to a small diner.

When I pushed the slate glass door open, I could smell hamburger and French fries. I breathed deeply, as if I could get nourishment from the smell of food alone. I walked across the black and white tile floor and slid onto a stool. The waitress slapped a menu card on the counter in front of me and I studied it, looking for something cheap, then ordered a toasted cheese sandwich and a Coke.

I watched the waitress clear away dirty dishes and wipe the counter with a wet cloth. She wore a brown and white checked uniform with a little white apron and a waitress cap that sat just behind her blond bangs. She was about my age and on her uniform pocket was a pin that said, MARIANNE.

As I watched her carry plates to the other customers, I wondered where she came from and how she happened to be working in the little diner. The thought crossed my mind that maybe I could work there too.

When she brought my sandwich, I said, "I'm new in town and I'm looking for work. Do you know of any jobs around here?"

She reached under the counter for a newspaper, "Take this, you can check the want ads."

When I was back in the room, I circled every ad for jobs that might be possibilities. The next day I applied for all the jobs I had circled, but no one hired me. In the evening, I went back to the diner and Marianne asked if I'd had any luck.

I shook my head and said, "No luck today."

I ordered a bowl of chili and she gave me extra crackers.

When I paid her, she handed me another newspaper and said, "I noticed Lucca's restaurant on Washington Street has a help wanted sign in the window. It's a little Italian place about four blocks from here."

The next day I borrowed an iron from the lady at the reception desk and pressed my dress and raincoat, then went to Lucca's to apply for the job. When I told Nick Lucca I had experience working in a cafe kitchen in Linden, he hired me on the spot.

That evening when I told Marianne I had the job, she seemed happy for me so I asked if she knew where I could rent a room.

"Would you want to try rooming with me? It would help me if we could share the rent."

"I need something that doesn't cost much," I said.

"Have another cup of coffee and I'll take you to see my room when I get off."

When the diner closed, Marianne wiped the counter and cleaned the pie case while I filled the sugar bowls and napkin holders to help her out.

We walked to a big square house on Barber Street where she had an upstairs room. When I saw her unmade bed, the stacks of clothes on the chairs, and piles of shoes on the floor, I wasn't sure I could live with Marianne. I had gotten used to having my room neat and clean and untidy places made me nervous.

I hesitated only a moment, then knowing I couldn't afford a room of my own, I said, "I'll bring my stuff over in the morning."

Lucca's was a small place on the corner of Washington and Euclid. The front door opened into a room with a bar along one side and booths along the other wall. A second room was filled with tables covered with red and white checked table cloths. Maria Lucca was in charge of the bar and dining room and her husband, Nick, was head cook and managed the kitchen.

I was one of four cooks and because I was the youngest and the only girl, everyone called me "Cookie". I liked working in the kitchen that smelled of garlic, oregano, and cheese and was always warm from the steaming pots of boiling pasta. The time I'd spent watching Tony's mother cook Italian food and my experience working with Kate in the cafe kitchen had been good training. My job was cleaning, peeling, and chopping vegetables for Nick's sauces and setting up the salads at meal times. I learned to make a delicious vinaigrette dressing and even Nick said I got the seasoning just right.

I began to believe cooking was my hidden talent Kate had mentioned in the Tarot reading. I figured I'd work for Nick and learn all I could, then become a chef someday. But something happened that changed my mind.

It was closing time on a Friday night and I had wrapped the mixed greens and just finished capping the wine vinegar and the olive oil when Nick sidled up to me.

"Cookie," he said, holding out an enamel bowl. "I'll be needing a dozen onions first thing in the morning."

I thought about the dark, smelly basement and the dimly lit storeroom where the onions were kept. It was scary in daylight and I didn't want to go there at night, but I couldn't say no to my boss. I took the bowl and went down the steep stairs.

The storeroom door creaked when I pushed it open. I groped for the switch to turn on the light, only a bulb dangling on a wire from the ceiling. I squinted my eyes, searching for the big orange mesh bags I knew the onions came in. When I found the onions and bent over to fill the bowl, I heard footsteps behind me and before I could straighten up, felt a hand on my butt. I spun around and locked eyes with Nick.

He was standing between me and the door with a funny little grin on his face.

I drew in my breath with surprise but I didn't scream. I didn't make a sound. I just had a strange feeling that this was another secret, like Father's secret.

Nick stepped toward me and I stepped back, almost falling into the bags of onions. He reached for me and said, "I'm not going to hurt you."

I had heard those words before. I remembered Father saying those exact words just before he raped me. Anger flashed through me. My scalp seemed to tighten and my whole body felt hot, as if it were lit from within.

"You bet you won't hurt me," I said and pulled my Chef's knife from my belt where I had put it just before going down the basement steps.

"Hey, wait a minute!" Nick said as he backed away. He hunched his shoulders and seemed to make himself smaller as he backed slowly out of the storeroom.

I stood there until my breathing was steady, then climbed the stairs. Nick was standing in front of the range. He took a step back as I thrust the bowl of onions toward him and said, "Here are your damn onions."

"Look Cookie," he said," Let's forget what happened

down there...and don't say anything to Marie. Okay?

I would have liked to have gone into the dining room right then and told his wife what he had done, and I would have liked to quit my job, but I couldn't leave until I found another one. At that moment I made up my mind that I would leave Lucca's as soon as I could.

I saved money while I worked at Lucca's. I didn't need to buy many clothes because I wore black and white checked cook's trousers, a white coat and puffy hat for work. I didn't need to buy much food because I ate many of my meals at Lucca's. I was saving money because I wanted to take classes. I knew I needed to learn a skill so I could get a better paying job. I would have to have a good income if I expected to get Rosie away from Father, and saving her from what had happened to me was the thing I most wanted to do. Rosie was still young, but I wanted to get her away from danger as soon as possible.

I had been in Indianapolis almost a year when I decided to enroll in a beauty school. I had always liked working with hair and the course could be completed in nine months. When I told Marianne my plans, she decided to enroll at the same time. We would go to school in the mornings and work at our restaurant jobs from 3:00 P.M. to 11:00 P.M. each day.

The day we registered, I had an interview with Goldie Gilmoure, the school director. She looked elegant sitting behind her desk, wearing a green tailored suit the color of new peas. Her make-up was flawless and her dark hair was swept back and fastened with tortoise shell combs. I glanced down at the navy blue skirt and white cotton blouse I was wearing and felt like a real hick.

I watched Miss Gilmoure read my application. Then she looked at me over the top of her half-glasses and said, "I don't see a copy of your high school diploma here."

My heart sank, but I looked her right in the eyes and said, "I graduated from high school in Chester, Missouri. I don't have a copy of my diploma because the school was destroyed by fire and the records were lost."

I didn't wait for her reaction. I pushed my tuition money across the desk toward her. She raised her eyebrows, hesitated, then picked up the money and stamped "Accepted" on my application.

Marianne and I left the beauty school office and walked sedately down the steps but once we were out of Miss Gilmoure's sight, we started jumping and giggling and hugging each other. We had both been accepted to the beauty school and I felt like a little country mouse who was going to make it in the city.

We started classes in September, so if all went well I would receive my beautician's license in the spring. I hadn't been in school for a long time and didn't like the physiology class. I wasn't interested in learning about the muscles and tendons of the head and neck, but I loved the practice class where we worked with hair.

We started by cutting and styling wigs on mannequins, learning to do layered cuts, one-length cuts, cap cuts, and petal cuts. We gave permanent waves and learned to tease and rat hair. We practiced arranging bouffant styles and elegant up-sweeps. At the end of each week there was a contest to see who could give the best haircut or fix the most glamourous French twist.

Marilyn Monroe's blond hair had made bleached hair popular, so we all wanted to practice using peroxide. Marianne offered to let me bleach her hair if she could bleach mine. I spent hours bleaching her hair. The chemicals stung my eyes and left my fingers stained, but the results were worth it. Her new silver blond hair complemented her delicate skin color and her heart shaped face.

Marianne's new hair style affected her whole head, inside and out. She smiled more, seemed happier, and less shy. It was then I recognized that liking what you see in the mirror can raise a person's self-confidence.

The next week I sat in Marianne's chair, waiting to be

transformed into a blond beauty. She followed each step carefully, but alas, the results were a disaster. My brown hair didn't give up its color easily and the peroxide left it stiff and egg yolk yellow. Even after the toner was applied it was still bright yellow with the texture of straw. All the next week I covered my hair with a scarf until Miss Gilmoure and Marianne worked together to dye it back to brown.

Finally, we were ready for our first day on the floor. We would be working on customers who were paying for their hair styles. My first customer was a lady with shoulder length hair who just wanted a trim. I swiveled her chair so her back was to the mirror, then sectioned her hair and started cutting. When I stood back and looked, I could see the left side was a little longer than the right side. I cut a bit off the left side only to find I had cut it shorter than the right side. I tried to get it even on both sides but the hair was piling up on the floor under the chair and the hair on her head was getting shorter and shorter.

When I was finished cutting, I turned the chair around so she could see herself in the mirror.

"LOOK WHAT YOU'VE DONE TO ME," she shrieked. "I'M ALMOST BALD!"

Miss Gilmoure heard the shouting and came rushing over to calm her.

"You have a good haircut and it's very becoming. You must have known you take your chances when you get a haircut at a beauty school."

"I'M NOT PAYING FOR THIS!" the customer shouted. She picked up her purse and coat and stomped out the door.

The next day I got a second chance. My customer was a woman with long, limp hair that gave her a tired and bedraggled look. I cut her hair carefully into a poodle cut and gave her a permanent wave. The soft curls all over her head set off her pixie features. She looked great and was pleased with her new look. I noticed she kept glancing in the mirrors and held her head high as she paid Miss Gilmoure. I felt wonderful. I had found I could do something that would make women feel good about themselves and I could earn a living doing it.

The more I learned about hairdressing the more I liked it. When I stood behind a chair I felt confident and in control, and I seemed to know what to do to please my customers.

I admired Miss Gilmoure and learned more than hairdressing from her. I tried walking like she did, with perfect posture and my chin held high. I checked her every outfit and watched the way she tied a scarf around her neck or placed a pin on the lapel of her jacket. I noticed how she spoke with customers, often touching them lightly on the shoulder, making each one feel special.

"You must learn the business end as well as how to fix hair, unless you want to work for somebody else all your life," she said.

I often stayed late so Miss Gilmoure could teach me how to order supplies and how to record the day's income and expenses in the ledger.

Marianne turned out to be a good roommate and my first real girlfriend. We wore each other's clothes and had lots of fun together. When we could spare the money we went to movies or the roller-rink, where we could rent shoe-skates and spend hours skating round and round to the throbbing music of a Hammond Organ. Marianne was a good skater, even graceful, and boys would ask her to skate in the couples-only-skates. They'd cross arms and hold hands as they'd glide around the rink while I sat on a bench on the side lines. I'd never had roller skates when I was a kid so skating was something I had to learn how to do.

Marianne liked to talk, especially late at night when the lights were off and we were side by side in bed. She told me all sorts of things, like how she lost her virginity in the hay mow. "I did it because I was curious," she said. "I didn't even like the boy."

I was shocked that she'd had sex if she hadn't been forced to do it, and it surprised me that she talked about it and never seemed ashamed. I never told her how my virginity had been stolen from me. The shame that clung to me like moss to the north side of a tree, kept me from talking about myself or my family. As far as Marianne knew, I had just appeared on the streets of Indianapolis out of nowhere, and didn't have a past.

Marianne invited me to go home with her for Christmas. We took the bus and her father and little sister, Elaine, met us in Bloomington. We crowded into the cab of the pickup truck for the ride to the farm. I was reminded of Father's old truck and I made a secret wish that my family would have a happy Christmas. I had mailed a package with two picture books to Rosie and sent a teddy bear to Carlo.

Snow was piled high where the snow-plow had cleared the narrow dirt road that led us through stands of timber and across an old iron bridge. It was fun to be in the country again and I thought of the poem, "Over the River and Through the Woods," that I'd learned in fifth grade. I was glad I was going to be with Marianne's family for the Christmas holiday.

"Here we are," Marianne said, as we stopped by a post with a mailbox perched on top of it. There was a blast of cold air as her father rolled down the truck window and leaned out to take the mail from the box, then put the truck in gear and turned into a long lane that led to the house. The fresh snow on the old yellow house and weathered barn made the farm look like a calendar picture.

"Oh! This looks like a Christmas card," I said.

We left our boots on the back porch, then got out of our coats and stood around the space heater in the front room while I met Marianne's mother and two brothers. Her brother, Dale, lived at home and worked on the farm, and Bob was a student at Ohio State. The whole family was so friendly that I felt right at home.

"Soup's on!" Mrs. Grant called. "It's our tradition to have soup on Christmas Eve."

"Sounds good to me," I said, and we all found places

around the long kitchen table.

Mr. Grant said grace and I noticed everybody crossed themselves, but I just sat with my head bowed.

The soup was delicious and the homemade bread was the same kind Momma made. I ate so much bread I couldn't eat the cherry pie Mrs. Grant had baked for dessert.

After we ate we all sat around the table a long time and the family talked, but I mainly listened. I looked across the table at Marianne's little sister, Elaine, who was thirteen, just the age I was when Father started bothering me. I glanced at her father sitting at the head of the table and wondered if he was capable of doing such a thing. Surely not, yet anyone looking at my father would never guess what went on behind closed doors at our house. I looked at Elaine's delicate face and sweet smile and hoped she didn't have a hidden secret like mine.

We moved to the front room and opened presents. I had brought a big box of Fanny Mae chocolates for the Grant family and a lavender and blue scarf for Marianne. We sang Christmas carols while Bob strummed his ukelele. I liked Bob's appearance. His blond hair and light eyes gave him the same approachable look Marianne had.

We went to midnight mass in a little country church. It was very plain for a Catholic church but the simple beauty of it, decorated with evergreen branches and candlelight, brought tears to my eyes. I didn't get much from the service because I was busy trying to follow when to kneel and when to stand. I think the Grant family were moved by the mass because everyone was very quiet as we drove back to their house.

Before we climbed the stairs to go to bed, Mrs. Grant heated water in a tea kettle and filled a hot water bottle for us. The upstairs was not heated and we undressed quickly and slipped between the icy sheets, stretching our legs to reach the warmth of the hot water bottle at the foot of the mattress that was stuffed with straw. We were three in a row, Marianne on one side and me on the other, with Elaine between us. I had never slept three in a bed and was worried about taking up more than my share of the space. I turned facing the wall and then felt Elaine snuggle up to my back. Marianne snuggled up to Elaine and I found that sleeping three in a bed is a good way to keep warm on a cold winter night.

Christmas morning Mr. Grant killed and plucked two fat hens. "No need to spend hard-earned dollars for turkey when we have all those chickens out there," he said.

Mrs. Grant cleaned the chickens and stuffed them with sage dressing, then started the giblets boiling in a pan on top of the stove. Marianne set the table while I watched her mother mix eggs, flour, and salt into noodle dough. Using a rolling pin, she rolled the dough into paper-thin sheets, then her stubby fingers rolled each sheet like a scroll. With a sharp knife she sliced the scroll, then shook the slices out into long noodles and dropped them into the bubbling chicken broth. I liked being in the kitchen with Mrs. Grant and in my mind I could see my own mother, in her apron, making noodles for Christmas dinner.

Bob, Marianne, and I were going to take a walk before dinner, but Marianne backed out at the last minute. I think she wanted to spend time with her mother and I could understand that.

Bob and I bundled up and trudged though the snow. As we crossed the pasture on the way to the creek, I noticed a beautiful farmstead with a large house, white board fences, and well kept buildings.

"Who lives in that house?" I asked.

"That's the Kaplan's place. They own a lot of farmland around here and Dad is just one of his hired men," Bob said.

"Oh." I said, surprised to see the difference in the two farmsteads. The Kaplan's house looked like a mansion compared to the Grant's house.

"That's the way it works, Roy Kaplan owns land and has the money to buy machinery, seed, and fertilizer so he's the boss. Dad knows as much about farming and works as hard as Roy Kaplan, but he has no money to back him so he'll be a hired man for the rest of his life. Being a hired man is a hard life. The cattle and hogs never give Dad a day off. Even today, on Christmas, he was up at five o'clock doing chores."

We came to a fence and Bob held the top wires down so I could step over it, then said, "Dad gets a monthly wage, the use of the house, a cow to milk, and a hog to butcher. It's been a struggle for him and Mom taking care of four kids on a hired man's wages. My dad and both of my grandpas have been hired men and it looks like Dale will follow in their footsteps, but not me."

I thought about Ralph, who had started helping Father with the church services, and said, "I know what you're talking about. My brother is following in my father's footsteps but I can't imagine why he would want to do that."

"Marianne should have gone to college but there was no money for it," Bob said, "I got a scholarship or I wouldn't be at Ohio State. I want to help Elaine if she wants to go to college, and I want to get my education so I can make a good life for a wife and family someday."

As we reached the creek Bob scooped up a handful of snow, pressed it into a snowball and threw it across the water hitting the trunk of a pin oak tree.

"Good throw!" I said

"I always wanted to be a ball player but I never had a chance to play sports," he said. " When I was a kid I always had to come home on the school bus to help with the chores. I didn't like living on a farm and felt deprived because we never had money for books and trips like the town kids did.

I guess I still resent having had such a poor background. I had a lot of catching up to do when I got to college. Anyway, I plan to make a different life and getting an education is the only way I know to do it."

"I had a poor background too," I said. "I didn't even go to high school."

"Well you're a smart girl and you'll do all right for yourself, I'm sure."

"I'm working and going to beauty school at the same time because I want to help my little sister have a better life than I had."

"That's really good...when families stick together and help one another," he said.

I liked Bob. He seemed like a friend. Yes, a friend, not a threat to me.

We turned back, following our footprints in the snow. As we passed the corn crib Bob said, "Want to climb to the cupola? You can get a good view of the farm from there."

"Sure," I said.

Bob slid the heavy door along the rusted track to open it. The corn had been shelled and hauled to town and only the smell of musty grain and corn cobs lingered.

"Only one person on the ladder at a time. I'll go first," Bob said as he climbed the wooden slats nailed on the wall that served as a ladder.

I followed Bob up the ladder and he took my hand and pulled me up the last step. Shafts of sunshine came through the narrow window, warming the small space even on the cold morning. I went right to the window to look at the lovely snow scene below. The rooftops of the house and buildings looked as if someone had frosted them with white sugar icing. I could see Bob's dad carrying buckets of feed to the hog house and the black Lab running circles around him. To the east I could see the creek and the path our footprints had made all the way to the barnyard.

Bob stood behind me, looking over my shoulder, and I

could feel his closeness. I turned toward him, my face only inches away from his. For a moment I thought he was going to kiss me and I wondered if that was why he had brought me up there, but he didn't kiss me. Instead he put a hand on my elbow and said, "Mom and Marianne must have the Christmas dinner about ready."

As I climbed down the ladder, I felt light and happy that Bob and I could talk and be friends and that he seemed to respect me.

At the bottom of the ladder, Ruff, the black Lab, was waiting for us.

"RACE YOU AND RUFF TO THE HOUSE!" Bob yelled, and we took off running for the back porch.

Late on Christmas afternoon, Bob took Marianne and me to the bus. As we said goodbye, Bob gave us each a hug and I didn't mind at all, although that was the first time since I left Tony that I had let a man get that close to me.

Marianne went to sleep as soon as we were settled in our seats. I didn't sleep because I was thinking about the things Bob and I had talked about. He was right about how families follow the same patterns and that it takes a special effort to break away from family limitations.

I leaned my head back and closed my eyes and thought about Rosie. I knew I wanted to make her childhood better than mine had been. If I could just get her to come live with me, I could keep her safe from Father. I could read books to her and teach her all I know...and best of all, Rosie and I could be a family.

Marianne and I were happy and excited the day we received our beautician's licenses and rushed down to Woolworths' to buy small black frames for them. Miss Gilmoure wrote a letter of recommendation for each of us and I was hired to work at the Beauty Salon in Ames department store. I had my own space: a mirrored wall unit with a cabinet to store my supplies and an adjustable chair. I put my scissors, combs, and brushes into a drawer and hung my license on the wall and started work.

The first few weeks my time was filled with walk-in customers but before long some women started asking for repeat appointments and my schedule was soon filled with regular clients. I tried to find the best hair style for each personality and I often gave suggestions on how to arch their eyebrows or what shade of lipstick would look best with their complexion. I smiled when I saw my clients sneaking looks at themselves in the mirrors, pleased with what they saw.

Some women go to a hairdresser for more than a hair style, they like the touch of a hairdresser and like to feel taken care of. Others want someone to talk to and confide in, and somehow, the feel of warm sudsy water on their scalps makes women relax and open up. Many of my customers have told me things they'd never tell their sister or best friends, or even their priest. I give my clients my undivided attention and listen to their troubles but never give advice.

One thing I've learned is that nobody has a perfect life. No matter how smart or rich or beautiful a woman is, she still has some kind of a problem. Some women come in and ask me to arrange their hair to cover bruises, cuts, and black eyes. They always say they ran into a door or had a bad fall on the stairs, but I know that's not what happened. I fix their hair and apply cover-up makeup to their bruises. We talk about this and that, but they never mention what really happened. Their secrets are just like mine...too shameful to talk about.

My customers knew I'd work early or late to accommodate them and they paid me well. In the first year I saved enough money to buy a car and rent an apartment of my own. I moved into the upstairs of a lovely old house on Grand Street that had high ceilings, beautiful woodwork, and hardwood floors, something like Mrs. Andrews' house in Roundhill. I spent every Sunday in second hand stores and at garage sales looking for furniture that I could paint or refinish. I painted a bed white, made a pink bedspread and curtains for Rosie's room and filled a bookcase with books and toys. Finally I had a place for Rosie but I had to figure out how to get her away from Father.

One Sunday I sat down with a pencil and lined tablet on my lap, writing, crossing out, and writing again...trying to find the right words. After several tries, some with demands and some with threats, I remembered that Momma always said you can catch more flies with honey than with vinegar.

I wrote: *Dear Folks, I'm sorry I haven't seen you for so long, but I've been busy getting my beautician's license. I now have a good job and a nice apartment. I'll have a week's vacation the first week in August. I think it would be wonderful for Rosie to visit me at that time. It would be a good experience for her. I could take her to the zoo, to Turkey Run State Park, and I promise she won't miss Sunday School and church. Please let her come. Lilly*

I waited two long weeks for a reply, then a postcard came, saying Ralph could bring Rosie to visit me. Father would put them on the bus in Lexington and I could pick them up in Indianapolis.

Rosie had been on my mind every day since I had left her but I hadn't realized how much she would have grown and changed since I had seen her. On the day they were to arrive I was at the bus terminal early, pacing around the terminal that still looked and smelled the same as it had two and a half years before, when I had arrived on the bus from Linden.

When Ralph and Rosie stepped off of the bus I couldn't take my eyes off of Rosie. She was no longer a baby and the only thing about her that was the same was her big, round, navy blue eyes.

I rushed toward her, wanting to take her in my arms but she hung back, hiding behind Ralph.

I knelt down so my face was level with hers and said, in my softest voice, "I'm Lilly, your sister. I used to call you Rosie Posy. Don't you remember?"

She held tight to Ralph's leg, but she smiled and I recognized the same smile I'd seen in the mirror all my life. My heart almost burst with pride that such a beautiful child had come from my body.

When we got back to the apartment, Rosie ran from room to room and was surprised to find books and toys in the room where she would sleep.

That evening I packed a picnic and we piled in the Studebaker and went to Canterbury Park. Ralph pushed

Rosie in a swing, then she climbed the monkey bars and hung from her knees on the trapeze. I decided we would go to Montgomery Wards the next day to buy shorts for her. I had looked through the clothes Momma sent and there were only dresses.

After we ate, Rosie ran to the slide and followed some other children up the ladder. I looked across the picnic table at Ralph. He wore dark pants and a white dress shirt with the cuffs rolled up above his wrists. I wanted to tell him he should let his hair grow longer and get some tee shirts and blue jeans, but thought better of it. Maybe I would tell him later in the week.

"I know you've been helping Father with the church services, but have you decided what you are going to do?" I asked.

"I don't know. Father wants me to see if I can get in to Moody Bible Institute."

"Do you want to do that?"

"I guess," he said, shrugging his shoulders.

I was sure that Ralph's going to a Bible Institute to learn to be a preacher was more Father's idea than Ralph's, but I decided to drop the subject because Ralph would have to find his own way to deal with Father.

I started gathering up the remains of the picnic. "Call Rosie," I said. "We'll stop at the Dairy Queen for dessert."

I was glad I'd left a light on because it was dark when we climbed the stairs to the apartment. Rosie was tired so I helped her with a bath, folded back the pink bedspread, and turned out the light. It was a warm, clear night and moonlight shore through the windows. I could see her little head with her honey-blond hair fanned out against the pillow. Tenderness rose in my chest. More than anything in the world, I wanted to love and protect her. I had dreamed of the day I would see her again and the dream had come true.

I leaned over and kissed her smooth cool forehead and whispered, "Good Night."

As I turned to leave, she said, "Who's going to listen to my prayer?"

"We could say our prayers together," I said. "I bet I know the prayer you say."

"I can say it. I know all the words," she said.

I listened as she prayed, *"Now I lay me down to sleep, pray the Lord my soul to keep. Thy love guard me through the night, wake me with the morning light. Amen."*

Rosie turned onto her side. "Now lie down beside me and hug me and touch me like Father does," she said.

My hand went to my chest and I sucked in a long breath as the memory of Father's hands touching me flashed in my mind. My throat went dry and my cheeks began to burn as alarm raced through my body.

"Show me where Father touches you," I said.

As Rosie lifted her nightgown, my worst fears were realized. The day, that had seemed like a dream come true, turned into a nightmare. My heart raced and a feeling of nausea rose in my throat. I could barely manage to whisper good night before leaving the room.

Standing outside Rosie's door, fresh anger toward Father filled me. I had lived with the shame and sorrow of what he had done to me and I had kept the secret. I had been too young and felt too unworthy to fight him when he hurt me, but I would find the strength to fight him for Rosie's sake. I felt as fierce as a mother bear protecting her cub and would do whatever I had to do to keep Rosie safe.

I hurried into the living room where Ralph was watching Oral Roberts on TV.

"TURN THAT OFF!" I yelled.

"What's the matter?"

"Did you know Father's been touching Rosie at night

when he puts her to bed?"

"How would I know anything about that? he said.

"IT'S YOUR BUSINESS TO KNOW ABOUT THAT!" I shouted. "You can't just turn your head like you and Momma did when he hurt me. Do you want her to end up with Father's baby, like I did?"

Ralph's face lost its color and he sat still as stone, his hands gripping hard on the arms of the chair. His voice was low and quivering when he finally spoke. "You had Father's baby? Do you mean that Father is Rosie's father?"

When I nodded my head, he said, "I never knew that. I thought you'd gotten in trouble with some boy."

It was hard for me to understand how he couldn't have known...hard for me to accept that he had believed the pregnancy was my fault and that Father was blameless. The buried hurt and pain bubbled up and hot tears rolled down my cheeks.

Ralph came across the room and put his arm around my shoulders, but I shivered and brushed him away. Having him close was too much like having Father near me.

In between sobs, I said, "Now do you see why I worry about Rosie being around Father? I'm going to keep her here. Will you help me?"

"You must be crazy! He'll never stand for it! He'll come get her."

'I'll cope with him," I said. "What I want you to do is to leave Rosie with me, and when you get home, tell Father she'll be staying with me from now on. Will you do that for me?"

"I'll tell him but you know it won't do any good."

On Saturday I took Ralph to the bus terminal. He hugged Rosie before he hopped on the bus and Rosie and I stood waving goodbye as the bus left for Lexington.

Later that evening, after I had read Rosie a story and she was asleep, the phone rang. It was Momma, her voice breaking and choking as she begged, "Please, Lilly, bring Rosie home. We love her. She loves us. She belongs with us. Please bring her back."

"I'm sorry this is going to hurt you, Momma, but I'm doing this to protect Rosie. You know you weren't able to keep Father away from me, and you won't be able to keep him away from her either."

I listened to Momma sob and I couldn't help but feel sorry for her. Then I realized Father had asked her to call to get my sympathy. It was so like him to use somebody else to get what he wanted.

"Let me talk to Father!" I said.

When Father came to the phone he said, "Lilly, what's all this foolishness you're talking? Rosie can stay one more week and then I'll come get her."

"Listen to me carefully, Father. Rosie is my child and I want her with me. She's going to start school here. Don't give me any trouble. If you do, I'll go to the police and report you for what you did to me. I'll let every church in the Midwest know what happened, and you'll never preach another sermon! Do you understand?"

I slammed the receiver down. I knew that was just the first battle of the war between Father and me.

The next week Rosie went to a playgroup each day while I worked. She didn't talk about Momma or Father and never asked about going back to them. We had settled into a routine and I was beginning to relax and believe that maybe Father realized that it would be better for Rosie to be with me.

On my Monday off, as Rosie and I came out the door on our way to the A&P, I heard a voice call, "ROSIE!" Before I knew what was happening, Father was squatting on the lawn and Rosie was running into his arms.

"DON'T TOUCH HER!" I screamed, but it was too late. Rosie was hugging Father.

I stood stock still, my heart pounding, my breath coming fast as Father glared at me over Rosie's shoulder, his eyes as cold and gray as steel.

"We can't talk out here. Come inside," I said.

We climbed the stairs and Rosie took his hand so she could show him her room.

"Rosie," I said, "you play here in your room while I talk to Father."

Father and I went into the living room and he sat down in the green arm chair. He was wearing a black suit and string tie, just what he had worn when I last saw him on the night I ran away with Tony. I couldn't help but wonder if that was the same black suit and if Momma still polished his shoes for him. I noticed the lines on his face had deepened and there were a few gray hairs at his temples.

I willed myself to be strong and tried to keep my voice steady as I said, "I don't know why you're here. Rosie is staying with me."

"Now Lilly, I came because Rosie belongs with Momma and me. She's used to your momma taking care of her and she loves us. It's not fair to uproot the child."

"Rosie is my daughter. I appreciate you taking care of her when I couldn't but now I want her with me."

"I'll tell you what we'll do...we'll let Rosie decide," he said. "Let's let her choose where she'd rather be."

"Oh no," I said. "A child of six is not old enough to make that kind of decision. Rosie is my child and she's staying with me and that's final!"

He sat staring at me, then looked down at the floor and said, "I know you're still mad at me about what happened. I would never do a thing like that again, believe me. You would never have to worry, I would never touch little Rosie, I swear."

"You bet you'll never touch her. I'm going to see to

that."

"Look here, Lilly, she's as much my child as she is yours. You went off and left her and gave up your rights to her."

"The things you did to me, drove me away."

"Come on, girl, you were asking for it. It was better it was me that taught you to be a woman instead of some punk boy."

The anger that had been simmering within me came to a full boil. Suddenly I wanted to cry all the tears I had choked back and say all the words I had swallowed. I wanted him to know how much he had hurt me and I wanted to hurt him too.

"YOU RUINED MY LIFE!" I shouted, the words coming fast, tumbling out, "What you did to me was abnormal and against the law! It's incest! I'll fight you! I'll go to the police. I'll get a lawyer. You'll never get another job preaching."

"Now, now..." he said, his voice quivering." Rosie was born to you but Momma has been her mother since the day she was born. She knows Momma and me as her family and you must not tear her away from us. If you love her, you must give her up."

"Remember the story of King Solomon?" he continued. "Two women claimed to be the mother of the same baby. The wise king offered to cut the baby in half so each one could have a part of him. The real mother offered to give the baby to the other woman rather than see the baby hurt. She showed her love for the baby by being willing to give him up. It will hurt Rosie to be taken from us. You can show your love for her by giving her up. If you love her you must give her up!"

"NO," I cried. "If you love her, you must give her a chance for a normal life."

"Let me see her again! Let me talk to her!" he demanded.

"IF I HAVE MY WAY, YOU'LL NEVER SEE HER

AGAIN," I shouted. "YOU ARE EVIL!"

He jumped up, towering over me, and as I looked up at his narrowed eyes and clenched jaw, I realized he might be dangerous.

I stood up and controlling my urge to run, walked slowly to the door and threw it open.

"Get out!" I said, trying to keep my voice even. "Leave or I'll call the police."

I stood by the door as he walked slowly toward me, his fists clenched.

He stopped in front of me and put his nose close to my nose and said, "You were taught to honor your father and your mother. You have defied me. You have sold your birthright for a mess of potage. I disown you."

He stomped outside.

I closed and locked the door and leaned back against it, my whole body trembling. I could hardly believe I had stood up to Father, had told him he had hurt me. I had finally told him how he had made me feel.

But what next? Would he leave Rosie and me alone? I was filled with doubts. Maybe we should move, run away to some place where Father couldn't find us. I glanced around the apartment. The sunlight streamed through the west windows, warming the golden oak floor. I looked at the drapes I had made, the rich patterned rug, and the Sunflower painting I had bought at a garage sale. This was our home, a real home. I would not run away again. I had stood up to Father once and I would do it again...as many times as I had to.

I went to the bathroom and splashed water on my face. When Rosie heard me she came in and asked where Father had gone.

"He's gone back to Kentucky," I said. "I think he has a sermon to write."

"Can we go to the store and buy some Oreo cookies now?"

"Sure."
I reached out and took her small hand in mine.

Father

Momma

Ralph

Lilly

Rosie

Mrs Andrews

Trudy Andrews

Mrs Andrew's House

Tony

Mama Belcanti's House

Mama Belcanti and Baby Carlo

Carlo, 3 years old

Marianne

Miss Gilmore and Marianne

Part Two

ROSIE
FINDING HER OWN WAY

"It is our challenge to create a society in which all citizens are equal. We must grant Civil Rights to every American," I said, as I finished my rebuttal and sat down, my heart pounding. I glanced at Mr. Simon, our debate coach. He was smiling and that was a good sign.

When the points were tallied, the judge announced, "The winner is Central High School, Indianapolis."

I let out a scream and Dale and I hugged then pulled apart, embarrassed that we had touched each other. The competition had gone down to the last debate but all our work had paid off....we'd won the state contest. A photographer snapped our picture and asked for the correct spelling of our names and the names of our parents.

My name is really Rosie Page and my father is Reverend Clifford Page, but I go by the name of Rosie Belcanti because I live with my sister, Lilly Belcanti. I've lived with Lilly since I was six years old so I can stay in one school instead of moving from place to place with our parents.

We haven't seen our mother and father in a long time because Lilly and Father had a falling-out and don't speak to each other. I don't know what was such a big deal that they've stayed mad for years. I've asked Lilly many times but she says she'll tell me later, always later. Even my older brother Ralph, who is usually easy to talk to, clammed up when I asked him. I wish they would make up so I could see my parents sometime. I remember Mama baking cookies for me when I was little and I still have the rag doll she made for me.

I'd like to visit my folks in the summer like Carlo visits us. Every summer he comes to Indianapolis on the bus and stays for two weeks. It seems strange that Carlo is my nephew since I'm only three years older. He's a big boy, taller than me, but he acts like a baby. Lilly always takes her vacation from work while he's here and she gives him whatever he wants. Lilly says, "What do you want for supper, Carlo? Where would you like to go, Carlo? What can I buy for you, Carlo?" Sometimes I get angry seeing her wanting to please him so much.

I'm looking forward to the end of school. Now that I'm sixteen maybe I can get a summer job...that is if Lilly will let me out of her sight. She'll probably be afraid that I might look at a boy or that a boy might look at me. She's such a prude, always saying, "Pull down your skirt. Keep your knees together. Never sit on a boy's lap. Never let a boy get you alone!" Sometimes I wonder if she's afraid of men. She's so pretty, she could have a boyfriend but she definitely doesn't want one.

She doesn't know I like Kenny Porter. He's on the basketball team and the cutest boy in our class so I try to get him to notice me. After Lilly leaves for work each day, I stuff bobby socks in my bra so I look older and sexier, then I put on eye makeup, and roll over the top of my skirt to make it shorter. I know Lilly doesn't like for me to wear eye makeup and short skirts but I don't see any harm in it. She's just too old fashioned and can get upset about the smallest thing.

One afternoon last fall, Linda and Debbie came home

with me after school and Debbie had a joint in her purse. We opened every window in the apartment and each of us had just a few hits but the minute Lilly came home and opened the door she started yelling, "WHAT'S GOING ON HERE?" Then she answered her own question with,"YOUV'E BEEN SMOKING POT!"

She sat all three of us on the couch and cross examined us like she was Perry Mason.

"Who brought marijuana into this apartment?"

" I did," Debbie answered, making her voice so low she could hardly be heard.

"Where did you get it?" Lilly demanded.

Debbie was really squirming, but she said, "Somebody at school gave it to me."

"Did you pay for it? Was someone selling marijuana at school?"

"No, no. Somebody gave it to me, somebody I don't know very well. I can't remember his name."

"I'll bet!" Lilly said, her voice shrill with anger. "You two go on home. Get out of here and don't come back."

Linda and Debbie scurried toward the door and Lilly called after them, "I'LL BE CALLING YOUR PARENTS TO TELL THEM ABOUT THIS."

As soon as the door slammed behind them, Lilly started on me.

"How could you have done that after all I've told you about drugs? I've told you a million times that you must never get started with drugs!"

I was still thinking about Linda and Debbie instead of what Lilly was saying to me, so I said, "Please, Lilly, don't call their parents. If you do, Linda and Debbie will hate me forever."

"Rosie, my dear Rosie," she said, "I'm not responsible for Linda and Debbie. You are the one I care about. I love you more than I love myself and I want you to have a good life."

"I know, I know..."

"Promise me you won't hang around with those girls anymore. This is for your own good."

"I promise."

Lilly wants me to be perfect and have all the things she didn't have when she was a girl. She buys really nice clothes for me, better than the other girls have. Looking good means everything to Lilly. Every Thursday night, like clockwork, she plucks her eyebrows, gives herself a facial, sets her hair, polishes her shoes, and straightens her closet. I don't polish my shoes and I like my hair long and straight, but I do try to keep my closet neat because I don't want to drive Lilly crazy. She wants me to get good grades and I always do. That's very important to Lilly because she expects me to go to college. She's saving money and hopes I'll earn a scholarship. I don't know what I want to be, I just know I don't want to be a hairdresser like Lilly.

One evening as Lilly slid a pan of bubbling hot lasagna from the oven and cut a square for each of us, she said, "How'd you like to take a little trip over Memorial Day?"

"Where to?"

"I was thinking it would be nice to go to Chicago."

"Do I have to?"

"It would be fun and it would be good to get out of Indy over Memorial Day when the city is crowded with race fans. We haven't been to Chicago for a long time and we could go to the Art Institute, shop on Michigan Avenue, and maybe see a play."

"Can Amy come with us?"

She poured herself a cup of coffee, put cream in it and said, "I want this to be just the two of us...I want to have time to talk. There are some things I want to tell you."

"Oh come on, Lilly. I already know about sex. My friends and I talk about that stuff a lot."

"Well, It's more than that, I really want to do this. Shall

I make a reservation?"

I mopped up the last of the tomato sauce on my plate with a piece of bread and said, "Okay, okay." I knew, from past experience, there was no point arguing if Lilly had made up her mind.

By the time school was out I was looking forward to the trip to Chicago. Lilly had made a reservation at the Ambassador East Hotel. We drove up early on Saturday morning and went to the hotel to check in. The suite of rooms looked like it belonged in a movie. Instead of wallpaper there was pale peach fabric on the walls and satin drapes hung from the ceiling to the floor. There was a bedroom with two huge beds, a marble bathroom, and an elegant little sitting room with a fireplace. On the table I found some books and magazines that advertised things to do in Chicago. When I saw the musical Hair was playing, I started to beg, "Please, please, please, can we go?"

Lilly rolled her eyes and then said, "If that's what you really want to do, I'll try to get tickets."

I stood close to her and listened while she phoned the concierge and ordered two tickets, then I gave her a big hug. This would be something special to tell my friends back in Indy. I was sure none of them had seen a rock musical.

Lilly insisted that we unpack and hang up our dresses before going to the Art Institute where we spent an hour in the Impressionist gallery. As I studied paintings by Monet, Renoir, and Cezanne, I noticed they seemed to have found beauty in the most ordinary things...fields, haystacks, train stations, even kitchen utensils and fruit. Lilly stopped in front of a painting of a beautiful lady standing in a field of flowers, wearing a long white dress and holding a green umbella.

"Wouldn't it have been fun to have lived in a time when women wore long dresses and carried parasols?" she said.

"I love long dresses. I'll be having one for the prom."

"So you will," Lilly said and moved to the next painting.

Something about Lilly's voice told me she had regrets about never having had a beautiful long dress or gone to a prom. She never went to high school and she told me that when she was young she wore clothes that Father brought home from the church mission boxes. She'd get tears in her eyes when she talked about going to school in hand-me-downs that were out of style and didn't fit properly.

The sun was bright when we came out of the Art Institute and Lilly snapped a picture of me on the steps before we walked to the Loop. We went to the Walnut Room in Marshall Field's and had chicken salad and Frango mint pie for lunch. Lilly bought a pair of blue shorts and a matching tee shirt for me, then insisted on buying me a dress, even though I didn't need one.

When we got to the theater that evening, the lobby was crowded with young people and the air was thick with the smell of pot. Lilly hurried me to our seats. The lights dimmed and I heard a gong sound from the back of the theater. I turned around and saw members of the cast coming forward through the audience, making their way to the stage. This was such a strange beginning and it captured everyone's attention.

I was immediately caught up in the show. The actresses had long flowing hair and were beautiful in long flowered skirts and gauzy blouses. The music was loud and the dancing was wild and free. I could feel energy coming from the stage as though there was a movement to make the world a more free and tolerant place.

After the show, we stopped for dinner at a little restaurant on Oak Street. While we waited for our food, Lilly said, "Well, I'm not sure the show was worth the price of the tickets. I couldn't see any plot to it, and I think the nudity was uncalled for. I don't know why they had to play that music so loud."

I didn't say anything but I thought it was strange that although Lilly was only fourteen years older than me, her way of thinking was old, more like my teachers.

Later, back at the hotel, I couldn't get to sleep because the words and music of "The Age of Aquarius" played over and over in my head.

The next morning Lilly ordered breakfast in the room and we sat at the little table by the window. The May sun spotlighted the breakfast tray, making it look like the still life paintings we had seen at the Art Institute.

Lilly waited until I had finished the little pot of hot chocolate and then said, "Rosie, we need to talk. There's something I want to tell you."

She sat facing me, the light behind her, and I could see dark circles under her eyes. I wondered if she'd had trouble sleeping too.

She sat on the edge of her chair leaning forward and her voice sounded hoarse as she said, "I want to tell you something about our family. It's something I should have told you a long time ago but the time never seemed right."

Lilly was rubbing her hands together and looking down at the floor as she said, "I know this will be a shock, Rosie, but it's something you must know sooner or later. I'm not your sister. I'm your mother."

Lilly was my mother? She must be kidding; it couldn't be true. But...Lilly wouldn't kid about a thing like that.

"Are you telling me that Momma isn't my mother?"

"I'm telling you that I'm your mother." Her voice was trembling. "I was very young when you were born and at the time it seemed best for everyone to think Momma was your mother. Now it's time you know the truth. You are my daughter."

I was trying to figure out exactly what she was saying.

Lilly must have gotten pregnant when she was a teenager and didn't let anybody know about it. She must have had me, then went away and left me with her parents.

As I grasped this, I could feel the hot chocolate I had for breakfast backing up in my throat. Pain flashed through me. I felt hurt and rejection in every cell of my body. My heart speeded up and I couldn't seem to get enough air.

As soon as I caught my breath, I yelled at Lilly, "IF I WAS YOUR BABY, WHY DIDN'T YOU TAKE CARE OF ME? HOW COULD YOU LEAVE ME AND GO OFF AND MARRY TONY AND HAVE CARLO? IF I'M YOUR DAUGHTER WHY DIDN'T YOU TELL ME? HOW COULD YOU HAVE LIED TO ME YEAR AFTER YEAR?"

"Please, Rosie, try to understand. I was younger than you are now and I couldn't take care of a baby. It was better for you to stay with our folks until I could afford to come back for you. You were never out of my mind. It was always my goal to have you with me."

"But...what about Momma?"

"She's your grandma and Ralph is your uncle, not your older brother."

"And my father, who's my father?"

Lilly sat for a long time before she answered. "I really didn't want to get into that today, but I can see it's better to get this all out in the open right now. I know you don't want any more surprises waiting for you."

Lilly stood up and started pacing back and forth across the room. "Rosie, there are some things that happen in families that should never happen. Sometimes one person, a powerful person, takes advantage of a weaker one. That's what happened in our family. I was young and innocent and my father came into my bed at night and took advantage of me."

I was beginning to get the idea, but I asked, "What do you mean?"

Lilly's face was white, and tears were puddling in her eyes and trickling down her cheeks. "My father used me for sex from the time I was thirteen until I was sixteen. I ran away from our family when I was your age because that was the only way I could get away from him. It was a terrible thing, but it happens in more families that you would think. There's a name for it. It's called incest and sometimes it results in the birth of a child."

Lilly blotted her eyes and her voice was so low I could hardly hear her as she said, "That's what happened to me, I became pregnant."

I thought about that a minute and then stammered, "Are...are you telling me that I'm the child of you and Father? Was I born because you and your own father slept together?"

"Rosie, you are the one good thing that came out of the whole mess. Our family loved you and were happy to have you. Who your mother and father were didn't matter."

"Say it," I sputtered, "Go ahead and say it. I DON'T HAVE A NORMAL FAMILY! I'M DIFFERENT FROM EVERYBODY ELSE!

Lilly reached for another Kleenex and said, "Rosie Posy, We're a family and you know I love you! You're the one person who gives my life meaning...the one thing I've hung on to. If it hadn't been for you, I might not be alive today. My life hasn't been easy and there were times when I felt like giving up, but I knew I had to survive so I could take care of you. I was determined to get you away from Father and save you from the same thing happening to you."

I just sat there, stunned with disbelief. I was so shocked that I didn't even cry. This was like a nightmare, a nightmare that couldn't be true. Then I looked at Lilly's contorted face and I knew I had to believe her.

Anger built up within me until I thought I would explode. I was furious that such a terrible thing could happen. I was enraged that the man I had known as my father had done such a hateful thing. I was angry that Lilly had left me and had let me think my grandmother was my mother. I was incensed that this had happened to me. Why me? I had not made it happen and I could do nothing to change it. I felt that I had fallen into a dark pit that I hadn't even known existed.

I sat at the table staring at Lilly as if I had never seen her before.

"Please understand," Lilly pleaded.

When I didn't respond, she said, "Let's get some fresh air. Get your coat, Honey. Let's go down by the lake and walk while we talk."

It was a cool May morning and the wind was blowing off Lake Michigan. I let the wind bite my face and whip my hair. I was hurting so much on the inside that I wanted my body to hurt too. I started running as fast as I could along the lake shore. I ran and ran. Lilly ran too but she couldn't keep up and dropped behind, finally slowing to a walk. I looked back. I wanted to get away from her so I kept running for over a mile. Then, near exhaustion, I collapsed on a bench. As I sat gasping for breath, waves of anguish and despair rose and fell within my chest. I felt I had lost part of myself that I would never find again.

As I looked back, I saw Lilly making her way toward me and at that moment I hated her. She had caused my world to crumble. All I could think about was running away and staying away from Lilly forever. I would have run away right then, but I didn't have the energy. When Lilly reached the bench, she sat down beside me and tried to give me a hug. I wouldn't let her touch me and I wouldn't talk to her.

"Come on, Sweetie," she said, "In spite of what happened in the past, we still have each other."

I didn't say anything but I was thinking, *Oh yeah, that's what you think!*

O n the next Monday, after Lilly left for work, I rode my bike to the library. I went right to the card catalog and looked up incest. The sound of the word made shivers go up and down my spine. There were only a few titles listed, but I found three books and the Webster Dictionary and carried them to the large oak table. I threw my jacket over the pile of books so no one could see what I was reading and opened the dictionary.

> Incest--*Sexual acts or inbreeding between individuals too closely related to be allowed by law to marry.*
> inbred--*an individual resulting from the mating of closely related patrents.*

"MY GOD! I'm inbred." I said, then glanced around to see if anyone was close enough to have heard me.

I opened one of the books and as I read, a gray cloud of depression seemed to settle around me. After five minutes of reading, I didn't want to know anymore. I grabbed my jacket, left the books on the table, and bolted for the door. When I was outside I looked around. The sun was still shining, the grass was still green, and the lilacs and peonies were still blooming. How could everything look the same as always when everything had changed for me ?

I dropped down on the library step, not trusting my wobbling legs to pedal me home. Karen Ames came up the walk carrying an armload of books.

"Rosie, hi," she said. "Did you have fun in Chicago?"

"Oh, we had a wonderful time."

I had always tried to tell the truth, but at that moment I knew that for the rest of my life I would lie, or do whatever I had to do, to hide the secret.

Finally, I found the strength to go home and have a peanut butter sandwich and a glass of milk. Outwardly, things didn't change much. Lilly and I made an uneasy truce. I rode my bike and played tennis in the park with my best friend, Amy and watched a lot of TV: "I Love Lucy," "Ozzie and Harriet," and "What's My Line?"

On the inside, I was upset and confused. I still wanted to run away but where could I go? Before, when I'd been mad at Lilly, I'd imagined myself running away to my parents in Kentucky but now I knew I would never go near my father.

I hung around the house a lot and one afternoon I wrote a letter.

Dear Abby,

I'm a sixteen-year-old girl and I've just been told that my parents are not who I thought they were. The person I thought was my sister is really my mother and her father is my father too. I'm inbred and I'm scared about that. I seem normal but can I have normal life? Will I be able to marry and have children?
Please answer soon. I read the Indianapolis Star *newspaper.*

I signed the letter *Girl with a Secret* and walked to the Post Office to buy a stamp and mail it before Lilly came home from work. I read the newspaper every day and watched for an answer, but if Abby ever answered my letter, I never saw it.

On Labor Day, I saw Kenny Porter at a party. He came over to the picnic table where I was sitting and said, "Come on, Rosie, let's dance."

"Sorry," I said, "I hurt my ankle playing tennis and can't dance." Lying was really easy. I didn't want to dance with him. I didn't want to get close to him or any boys.

Just as he was walking away I called after him, "Kenny, do you happen to have anything to drink with you?"

"Sure, Rosie." he said, and pulled a flask from his back pocket. He looked surprised as I took three big gulps. I choked and coughed but I kept it down. I was hoping it would numb me. I wanted it to blot out my pain and make me forget who I was.

On the first day of school I stopped at Blake's Market and bought a pack of Salem Menthol cigarettes. At noon I went across the street from the school to the corner where the smokers gathered.

I stood next to Steve Holloway and lit a cigarette, then said, "I want to get a little booze. Do you know of anybody who can help me?"

"Ask Rick Morton. He can always get it." Steve answered.

Just before the one o'clock bell rang, I asked Rick if he could supply me with some liquor.

"My older brother can get it for you, but you have to pay in advance."

"OK," I said as I dug a five dollar bill out of my purse. "Have him get a bottle of whisky for me."

A few days later Mr. Simon stopped me in the hall,

and said, "Rosie, you haven't signed up for the debate team yet."

"I'm not going to debate this year," I said, my mind foggy from the Jack Daniels I'd had at lunch time.

"We need you. The whole team needs you."

"I don't have time for it this year." Why tell the truth when lying was so easy?

20

The reason I signed up for watercolor painting was that I had heard it was a "goof off" class and that Mr. Alden never failed anyone. I was disappointed when I found out I didn't get into Mr. Alden's class but had been assigned to the new teacher's class instead. Miss Laurel didn't look like a teacher. She was young and attractive in her long flowing skirt and blouse in a flashy modern print. She wore the biggest silver necklace I had ever seen, long dangling earrings, and many bangles on her wrist.

The first time the class met, Miss Laurel instructed us how to set up our pallets. We squeezed the little tubes of paint, depositing globs of color into each well of our white plastic pallets. The paints had wonderful names: Alizarin Crimson, Windsor Violet, Ultramarine Blue, Naples Yellow, and Viridian Green.

An arrangement for the class to paint had been set up on a small table in the center of the room. A purple table cloth was draped over the table and on the cloth was a vase containing one red rose. We were to study the subject for a full ten minutes and then paint it in any style we chose.

I looked at the rose and decided to skip the vase and table cloth and just paint the blossom, stem, and three leaves. I dipped my brush into the water jar and then into the Alizarin Crimson paint and painted the petals. Then, forgetting to rinse my brush, I dipped into the Viridian green paint for the leaves. As the red and green blended, I found that red and green mixed together makes black. I had black leaves. The black paint started to run into the red paint on the petals. I liked the black so I added more green over the red and more red over the green. When I was finished I had a huge black rose with three black leaves on a stark white background. At the bottom, I wrote LONELY ROSE in black letters.

The last twenty minutes of class was critique time. When I hung my painting in front of the class, I listened for someone to snicker and I expected Miss Laurel to lecture me on keeping a clean brush and on preventing one color from running into another, but instead she said, "This painting is striking. It is very expressive and it speaks to me on an emotional level. Good work, Rose."

"That's cool, I've never seen a black rose!" Mike Long exclaimed.

"Rosie, I didn't know you knew how to paint," Melissa Cook said.

Miss Laurel chose twelve paintings to display in the case in the hall outside the Art Room and mine was one of them. Later, as I looked at my painting hanging in the hall, I realized that I had been so absorbed in painting that I hadn't thought of myself or my secret for the whole fifty minutes in art class.

At the end of the week Mrs. Simon called, inviting me to supper on Friday evening. "Simple Simon," as we liked to call him behind his back, and Mrs. Simon often had the debaters over for Friday night supper. I almost refused the invitation because I figured he probably wanted to try to talk me into debating again, but I hadn't seen any of the kids on the team for a long time and Mrs. Simon was a good cook, so I accepted.

When I got to the Simon's house I walked up the front steps and rang the bell. As I waited, I looked at my reflection in the long glass pane of the door and noticed that I had lost quite a bit of weight since school started. In fact, all I needed were some false eye lashes and I'd look a lot like Twiggy.

Mr. and Mrs. Simon both came to the door. I gave a bunch of daisies to Mrs. Simon and she went to the kitchen to put them in a vase.

"Where is everybody?" I asked.

"This is everybody," Mr Simon said, "We wanted to spend some time with you, Rosie."

I was really surprised and uneasy to be the only guest. We went to the living room and I sat on the couch, wondering what we would talk about.

Mrs. Simon came from the kitchen with little glasses of V-8 juice and a basket of cheese crackers.

"What classes are you taking this year?" Simple Simon asked.

I listed my classes and then Mrs. Simon inquired, "Which is your favorite?"

"Art," I answered. "Definitely art."

We moved to the dining room table and Mrs. Simon served a pot roast with carrots and potatoes and she had made her special brownies for dessert.

When she passed the brownies, I said, "No thanks, I'm too full." The truth was I had lost my appetite for sweets since I'd been drinking.

Mrs. Simon asked, "Would you like coffee?"

I wasn't used to drinking coffee but it seemed like the adult thing to do so I said, "Sure, I'll take it black."

After dinner Mr. Simon said, "Rose, I want you to know that I'm not going to try to persuade you to come back to the debate team, although I'd be happy if you did. This is not about that."

He shifted in his chair, leaned forward and said, "I've noticed a change in you, Rosie. I know your grades are slipping and I'd like to know what's going on in your life that's made you change. You're a bright girl and you have the ability to accomplish anything you want. I know you may think it's none of my business, but I can't stand by and let you throw yourself away."

I didn't say anything and then he continued, "If you have a problem, we want to help you, Rosie."

I still didn't want to say anything, but he and his wife just sat there in silence so I had to say something.

"I'm okay," I said. "It's just things are different this year."

"How is it different?" he asked. "Is it something at home or at school?"

"It's nothing. I can't talk about it. It's really nothing."

"Rosie, we can understand if you don't want to talk to us, but we have a very good friend who's a therapist. If you talked to her, she could help you. It would be confidential, she would tell no one."

"She's a shrink? Do you think I'm going crazy?"

"No, no. It's not that at all. I'm concerned about you because a sudden change of behavior can indicate a problem. Sometimes a therapist can help us understand the problem and lead us toward a solution."

"There is no solution to my problem," I said.

"There is some way to resolve every problem, even if it is just learning to accept it and live with it." he said. "I want to tell you something about our friend Elizabeth. We were in school together and she is about my age. She is a really neat person and I know you'd like her. She works with teenagers and their families all the time."

Families? I don't have a family, I thought.

I wasn't about to let him trap me into seeing a shrink so I said, "I must go. Thank you very much."

Simple Simon wasn't ready to give up. "We would be

happy for you and Elizabeth to meet here. You could use my study."

"I'll think about it."

As we all stood up, Mr. Simon gave me a card and said, "Here's our friend's name and number. I hope you'll call her. And give us a call if we can help in any way."

"Thanks for the nice dinner," I said.

I was glad to get out the door. When I was down the steps, I read the card:

Elizabeth Mason, Therapist.

I considered putting the little card in the trash can on the corner, but for some reason I stuck it in my jacket pocket instead. At least they hadn't suggested that I talk to a minister. That would have been a real joke.

I knew Lilly would find out about my drinking and I thought my grades would be the thing that would tip her off. When I saw two Cs on my report card I stuck it in my locker and left it for several days, then I signed Lilly's name on it and returned it to my home room teacher.

A couple of weeks later Lilly asked, "When is your report card coming?"

"Soon, I'm sure," I said. "Don't worry about it."

"I'm anxious to see how you're doing. You don't seem to have much homework this year."

As it turned out, It wasn't my report card that got Lilly's attention.

When I left school on Friday I saw Debbie and Linda waiting for their bus.

"Hey Rosie, we're going to Logan's Creek for a picnic on Sunday," Debbie said. "You should come. Kenny Porter will be there."

"I wouldn't go anywhere to see Kenny Porter or any boy," I answered.

"It'll be fun. At this time of year we'll have the park to

ourselves," Debbie said.

"Yeah, it'll be a blast," Linda added. "Rick Morton is giving us a ride out there and we're leaving at ten. Debbie and I'll get lunch stuff and the girls will chip in to pay for it. We won't have to worry about the drinks...the boys will bring those, if you know what I mean!"

I hadn't made up my mind about going to the picnic yet when Amy called Saturday afternoon to see if I wanted to play tennis on Sunday. I was bored with tennis, since we'd been playing all summer and fall, so I suggested that Amy go to the picnic with me.

"Okay. I can't play tennis by myself, so I might as well go," she said.

Sunday started well. Lilly slept late so I didn't have to tell her where I was going. I left a note saying Amy and I were going to a picnic but didn't mention that Linda and Debbie would be there. I didn't feel I had to tell Lilly the whole truth anymore, since I knew she had lied to me for years.

Rick picked us up and we drove into the country, past farm houses and fields of dry stubble left after the harvest. The gate to the park was chained and padlocked so we parked behind three other cars on the grass beside the road. We unpacked the car and lifted the lunch bags over the fence, then carried them down the lane toward the creek. As we came around the curve we saw a bunch of kids sitting on the top of two picnic tables that had been pushed together.

Someone yelled, "Here comes Rick and his harem!"

The park was beautiful, and as Debbie had predicted, there were no other people there. Although it was November, the sun was warm, the sky was a clear blue, and the leaves on the ground were crisp. I thought I might write a poem about the November day that didn't want to be cool and gray so it disguised itself as an October day. Then I wondered if I could disguise myself as a girl without a secret.

While Linda and Debbie put out the lunch, Amy and I walked down the dirt path that followed the creek to the back fence of the park. The creek was low and the thin silver line of water looked as if an artist had painted a long brush-stroke between the rocks in the creek bed.

We walked in silence, listening to the ankle deep leaves whispering under our feet, then Amy said, "Don't tell any-one, but I think my mom and dad may get a divorce."

"A divorce?" I said, shocked.

Amy's family had always seemed perfect to me. I had en-vied her because she had a mother, a father, and two brothers who all lived together.

Amy's voice quivered as she said, "I never thought this would happen to my family."

"Don't worry Amy, families aren't important. I've never had a real family and I d-don't c-care."

Even though I tried to sound strong, my voice broke and for just a minute I was afraid I was going to cry. I felt that old gray depression wash over me again. It was such a disappointment to find out that nothing was the way I had thought it was. The whole world seemed fake.

Neither of us said anything more and we walked back in a somber mood.

When we got to the picnic, everybody had started eat-ing without us and most of the food was gone. I didn't care because I didn't feel like eating anyway.

After lunch Rick went up the hill to his car and got more beer. The boys were drinking Budweiser and bottles of whiskey were being passed around. I had a drink, or maybe two.

"LET'S RAKE THE LEAVES INTO PILES," Debbie yelled. "LET'S HAVE A CONTEST TO SEE WHO CAN MAKE THE BIGGEST PILE."

We didn't have any rakes but it seemed like a good idea.

Everybody started raking leaves with their hands and gathering them in big piles, each group trying to make the biggest pile. We ran and jumped into the piles of leaves, shouting and laughing. More bottles were passed and the boys were drinking more beer. There was lots of giggling and falling into the leaves. Some of the boys and girls were covering themselves with leaves and making out, with only the leaves to hide them.

At least half of the kids were smoking. I don't know who dropped the match but we all stood fascinated as we watched a tiny finger of fire inch its way toward a pile of leaves. Whish!! The pile burst into flames and became a huge bonfire in seconds.

We were still all laughing and Rick shouted, "WHERE ARE THE MARSHMALLOWS?"

The fire was spreading from one pile of leaves to another and the flames were burning a path toward the picnic tables. We watched, horrified, as the dry wood of the old tables caught fire and exploded into flames.

"HEY, WE'VE GOT TO GET THIS OUT!" Kenny yelled. "HAS ANYBODY GOT A BUCKET?"

There were no buckets and some of the boys ran to the creek and got water in beer bottles.

The picnic tables were a scorching hot fire. Black smoke was billowing into the sky and the air was filled with the smell of burning wood and creosote. I was coughing and my eyes were stinging as I moved back, trying to get away from the intense heat.

"STOMP OUT THOSE PLACES WHERE IT'S SPREADING," Rick called to the girls. We all started stomping on the channels of fire that were creeping through the dry leaves.

Suddenly I heard a scream. The kind of scream you would hear in a nightmare. I spun around and saw it was Amy screaming. Amy's bell bottoms were on fire. Flames were encircling her legs. She stood, her eyes wide with horror, screaming. Then she started running. Rick ran after her. He tackled her and rolled her over and over in the grass. When the flames on her jeans were out, she lay on the grass like a crumpled rag doll.

I ran to her and dropped to my knees beside her. My whole body was trembling and my mouth was so dry that I couldn't say her name.

"SOMEBODY GET HELP!" Rick yelled.

Kenny ran up the hill to to go for help, but before he reached his car he met a fire engine coming down the narrow lane toward us. Someone from a farm nearby must have seen the black smoke and called the fire department.

When the fire was out, we all stood dumbfounded as we watched Amy being loaded into an ambulance. As it drove away, I knew I should have gone with her to the hospital. I guess I was just too shocked and scared to know what to do.

The police came and took down all our names and addresses. I thought about telling them my name was Page and that I lived in Kentucky, but I was scared to lie to the police. All the way home I was thinking that Amy would never have been out there if it hadn't been for me. I knew I would have to call her parents and I would have to go visit her in the hospital. I would have to tell her I was sorry. I was so sorry!

Rick dropped me off and as I climbed the steps I felt exhausted. I smelled of smoke and I was guilt-ridden about what had happened to Amy. When I unlocked the door and let myself in, I wanted Lilly to put her arms around me and comfort me like she used to do.

When I opened the door, Lilly took one look at me and said, "What the hell have you been up to?"

Before I could think of anything to say, the phone started ringing, ringing. Lilly turned to go into the kitchen to answer it and said, "You need a shower. Get cleaned up...

then we'll talk."

I was smelly and filthy so it took quite awhile to get clean and put on a clean shirt and jeans. I was still combing the tangles out of my wet hair when Lilly came into my room.

"Rosie Posy, what have I done wrong?" she asked, as she sat down on my bed, "I have struggled to give you a good childhood and I never thought you would get in trouble with the police! They called to tell me that you and eleven other underage boys and girls were drinking and set a fire in the park. Amy is in the hospital with third degree burns on her feet and legs."

"Oh, Lilly, I've got to go there. I've got to go see her. Will you go with me?"

"I'll go with you, but first you have to tell me what's going on with you. I can't believe how much you've changed. What is it, Rosie? I love you and I don't want you to slip away from me."

When she said that, I remembered that Mr. Simon had said, "I can't let you throw yourself away." Was I slipping away from Lilly? Was I throwing myself away?

I hesitated, then said, "It's what you told me in Chicago, that's what's wrong. Doesn't it bother you, Lilly?"

"Of course it bothers me! It bothers me every day of my life. Everything would have been different if I hadn't lived in fear of my father. From the time I was thirteen I dreaded every night because he might come to my bed. Then he got me pregnant when I was in eighth grade."

I sat quietly and listened to Lilly. I thought about how small I had been when I was thirteen and wondered what it would have been like for a little girl to worry about her own father coming into her bed to hurt her. I couldn't even imagine anybody being pregnant in eighth grade. I began to see that this wasn't just about me. It had affected Lilly even more than me. She had a rotten childhood and she would never be able to forget what her father had done. She'd been hiding that secret for years. But why, I wondered, didn't she tell someone and get help when it first happened.

"Why didn't you tell somebody?" I asked.

"Father warned me that if I told anybody he wouldn't have a job and our family wouldn't have money for food. They made me believe that our family staying together depended on my keeping the secret."

She cleared her throat and went on, "Things were different back then. We didn't have counselors at school and there was no one to tell. Father never wanted us to get close to anyone and we moved so often that I never had a friend or a teacher I knew well enough to trust. I never told anyone. I even kept the secret from Tony when I was married to him."

"Couldn't you have told Momma?"

"Momma knew, but she was no help."

The muscles in Lilly's jaw were twitching and her voice was tense as she continued, "I hate our father and it's best that you don't remember him very well."

"I remember Momma taking care of me when I was little," I said.

"As for Momma, she was such a weak person that she let Father dominate us all. I'm repulsed by both of them, especially since they pretend to be so religious."

Lilly kept smoothing the bedspread beside her as she talked, although it was already smooth.

"I had no control over my life for so long that now I've gone to the other extreme. Now I want to control everything and want things to be perfect. I can't help it. I know I go overboard, Rosie. I try to make everything just right. I've become such a perfectionist that I don't know how you put up with me."

I looked around my pink and white room that was pretty enough to be a picture in a magazine. Lilly had made my room a safe place for me. She had made a good home for us.

I reached out and touched her hand and she turned her hand over and laced her fingers between mine.

"I don't like to think about it and I don't like to talk about it," she said. "I didn't tell you for so many years because I didn't want you to worry about it. Now you need to know. I thought you were handling it but maybe we should get some help. I've been dealing with this for years and I know I should forgive and move on, but I just can't. It's the kind of thing that stays with you forever."

"What about me?" I said, choking on the lump in my throat. "If my friends find out they'll think I'm weird."

"Nobody is going to find out unless you tell them," she said. "If you do tell a friend, they'll understand that none of this was your fault. It happened before you were born."

I didn't mean to whine but my throat was tight and my voice came out higher than usual as I said, "But if I'm inbred my children will be freaks."

"Calm down," Lilly said, "The chances of you having problems like that are very slim. Just make sure you don't get involved with anyone related to us. That means Ralph's son, Aron. He's your cousin and he's also your nephew"

We both smiled as it seemed funny that Aron could be both my cousin and my nephew. I wouldn't ever marry him anyway. He was only ten years old and a real brat.

"Seriously," Lilly said, "We'll see Dr. Curry and get his opinion, but I think you have nothing to worry about unless you marry a relative."

Lilly stood, smoothed the bedspread again, and said, "Let's call the hospital and check on Amy."

I stood beside her as she called the hospital. When she finished talking on the phone, she said, "Amy is in stable condition but no visitors tonight. You can go see her tomorrow after school."

Lilly made scrambled eggs for supper but I had a nervous stomach and couldn't eat.

While we were still at the table, she said, "Listen, I'll talk to the police tomorrow, and I'll pay your share of the damage to the park if you promise me that you'll stay away from that bunch of kids. And...no more drinking. Can I count on that?"

"I'm really going to try to be better," I said.

"Good! Now you need to get to bed."

She gave me a hug.

On the way to my room, I stopped at the hall closet and slipped my hand into my jacket pocket. The card Mr. Simon gave me was still there.

Monday morning when I went to my locker I saw the old busy-body, Janice Hull, coming toward me.

"I guess you and your friends had quite a time on Sunday. I heard Amy Houser is in the hospital and may never walk again," she said.

I didn't answer her. I picked up my books and walked away.

"Please, please, God," I muttered under my breath. *"Don't let it be true."*

I hadn't prayed in a long time but I still remembered what I'd learned in Sunday School before I came to live with Lilly. I stopped in the restroom and after the bell rang and everyone cleared out, I went into a stall and folded my hands and bowed my head.

"Dear God, this is Rosie. I hope you haven't forgotten me. I am desperate and I'm asking for your help. Please let Amy be okay, and please let her forgive me. And don't let her parents get a divorce. I'll be forever grateful. Amen".

I walked into art class late but didn't get a tardy slip.

Miss Laurel pretended not to notice I was late and went right on explaining how to do a monochromatic painting. On the table was an empty brown paper grocery bag with lots of creases and shadows. We were to choose one color and mix three values from light to dark to use in the painting. Most of the class chose Yellow Ochre or Burnt Umber but I dug down in my paint box and found a tube of Indigo.

I mixed the paint with water and started with the lightest value, painting in the negative space around the bag. Then squinting my eyes I looked for the shadows on the bag and painted the shadow shapes with a darker value of Indigo. I left the white of the watercolor paper showing to represent the highlights where the light from the window shone on the bag. When I painted in the creases with the darkest Indigo, the shape of the bag seemed to jump out. I was pleased with the painting and decided to take it home to Lilly. Maybe she would put it on the refrigerator as she used to do with my pictures when I was in grade school.

When I left school I walked to Follett's book store and searched for a book to take to Amy. I wanted something special that would show her that she's my best friend. I found a pocket edition of *The Prophet* by Kahlil Gibran. It's filled with verses and on page 64, I found a verse about friendship. I looked for a bookmark to mark the page but they were all too big for the little book, so I took the pink ribbon from my hair, folded it, and placed it on page 64.

I took the number 99 bus that stops in front of the hospital and then went to the fourth floor. I was trying to be quiet but my Keds made a squeaking sound as I walked down the long, white corridor to room 433. I didn't know if I should knock, so I stuck my head in the door and saw Amy's mother sitting in a chair by the bed.

"Come in," Mrs. Houser called.

Amy looked so small lying in the bed with a frame and a sheet forming a white tent over her legs.

"Amy, are you all right? Are you going to be okay?" I asked, before I even said hi.

Amy gave me a small smile and her voice sounded weak as she said, "The doctor says my legs and feet will work as good as new, but they may never look like new again."

Mrs. Houser stood up and said, "I think I'll get a cup of coffee while you're here, Rosie." She kissed Amy on the forehead and said, "I'll be back soon."

When she was out of the room, I said, "Amy, I'm so sorry this happened."

I started to go closer to her bed but she said, "Don't look, Rosie, they aren't bandaged and they're really gross. There'll be scars. My legs will be ugly." She sounded as if the words were choking her and tears were streaming down her cheeks.

I handed her a Kleenex and said, "Hey, you can wear slacks and jeans and tights to cover them. You'll be able to walk and play tennis and nobody will look at your legs anyway."

"They're going to do skin grafting," she sobbed. "They'll take the skin from my stomach so it'll be scarred too. I'll never be able to wear a bikini again."

Before I could say anything she said, "Promise me you won't tell anybody at school that I'll have scars. Just say I'm going to be okay."

"Sure," I said, realizing I had one more secret to keep.

A nurse came in and I sat back in the chair while she took Amy's temperature. She noticed that Amy had been crying and wiped Amy's face with a damp cloth. She patted her shoulder and said she would come back with some juice.

After she left, I said, "The nurse seems nice."

"The nurses are nice, but I hate being here. I just want to go home. The food here is worse than school lunches."

"You missed a great lunch at school today," I said.

"Leather pizza and rubber Jell-o."

We both laughed. Then our nervous laughter grew into the giggles and we couldn't stop. Mrs. Houser was surprised to find us giggling when she came back.

I gave Amy the book and left, after promising that I would get her assignments from her teachers and bring her books to her.

While I waited for a bus, I decided that although I had resolved to stay out of trouble, I would break the rules and sneak a peanut butter and jelly sandwich to Amy the next time I came to see her. Surely the nurses wouldn't call the police if I got caught smuggling food into a hospital.

Amy's legs healed and nobody at school found out about her scars because she had special permission to wear sweat pants instead of shorts during P.E. class. I still felt bad that it had been because of me that she was in the park and got burned. We'd been best friends since second grade and I felt even closer to her since she'd trusted me with her secrets about her parents' divorce and her scars. I considered telling her my secret and I wish I could tell you that I did, but I didn't do it. I was just too ashamed.

Instead, we talked about college and being roommates. We both wanted to go to UC Berkeley ever since Miss Laurel told us about it. She'd gone to college there and during art class, while we painted, she talked about the beautiful campus, the coffee houses where there were poetry readings, Cody's bookstore, and the Amsterdam Art store that stocked every art supply you could ever want. She told us that from the hills of Berkeley you can see San Francisco and the Golden Gate Bridge across the Bay, and that the town of Berkeley is like an international community. Even the food is different from the food you can get in Indianapolis.

She showed us pictures of Sather Gate and People's Park,

where some of the protests were held. "It's a great university and a good place to go if you want to make a difference in the world," she said.

I knew what was going on in the world and wanted to make a difference. I watched Walter Cronkite every night and had seen pictures of Vietnam battlefields where a hundred Americans were being killed each week. I'd watched Civil Rights marches and Black Panthers marches. I saw riots at the Democratic Convention in Chicago and I'll never forget the shock of seeing the National Guards firing on students at Kent State...right in the Midwest.

Amy applied to UC Berkeley right away but I found out it costs a lot to go to school there. I knew Lilly couldn't afford the out of state tuition and room and board so I talked to the guidance counselor about scholarships. He said I should forget Berkeley and look at schools in Indiana, where I had a good chance at a scholarship. The thought of Amy and me being separated, her going to school in glamorous Berkeley and me staying in Indiana, was just too depressing. I thought my whole life was ruined so I asked Rick Morton to get more Jack Daniels for me and started hanging out with Linda and Debbie, smoking joints when we could get them. I sort of slid through the winter months and tried not to think about my future.

In the spring, Kenny Porter asked me to go to the prom with him. I shouldn't have mentioned to it to Lilly because when I told her, she said, "I forbid it!"

"But I've already accepted."

"You can just un-accept. The sooner you do it the better," she said.

I cried and pouted for days. I couldn't understand how Lilly could be so mean and wasn't sure I would ever forgive her.

The week before the prom Dale Horton, one of the guys on the debate team, asked me to go to the prom with him. Lilly said that would be okay, so at least I wouldn't miss out altogether. Lilly and I went shopping and I bought a beautiful formal made of pale pink satin with a net overskirt. Dale brought a gardenia wrist corsage when he came to pick me up and Lilly took our picture before we left.

The gymnasium was decorated with little tables and bright umbrellas, meant to look like a Parisian cafe scene. Dale and I sat at a table with Amy and her date, Tim Randall.

While the boys were gone to get punch from the refreshment table, Amy leaned across the table and whispered, "Look who just came in."

I gasped as Kenny Porter walked in with Linda. I didn't know they were interested in each other and Linda hadn't said a word about Kenny asking her to the prom. They sat at a table with Debbie and her date, Ned Sheets. I was wishing I was with Kenny and hoped he would at least ask me to dance, but he didn't. I noticed he kept disappearing from time to time and I figured he was going to his car to get a drink.

After the dance Amy, Tim, Dale, and I went directly back to our apartment, as I had promised Lilly we would. We sat on pillows on the floor and ate Lilly's special pizza, but I couldn't help thinking about the kids who had been allowed to go to post prom parties that would last all night.

Dale and Tim left about 1:00 A.M. and Amy and I got ready for bed. Amy stayed with me lots of nights since her parents' divorce. We were sitting on our beds, talking about which girls had looked best in their prom dresses, when the phone rang. Lilly answered it, then came to my room. I could see her shoulders sagging as she stood framed in the doorway, the light from the hallway behind her.

"There's been a terrible accident," she said. "A car with

four kids in it missed the curve on Ridge Road. Kenny Porter and Linda Sites were killed and Debbie Gardner and Ned Sheets are in the hospital in serious condition."

I sat frozen. I couldn't make my mind understand, couldn't accept that Kenny and Linda, who were dancing and laughing only hours before, could be dead.

We didn't go to bed or even try to sleep the rest of the night. We sat at the kitchen table drinking coffee. All I could think about was, that if Lilly had let me go to the prom with Kenny, it might have been me sitting in the front seat beside him when his car went off the road. It might have been me who was "dead on arrival" at the hospital.

I like to think I grew up some that night. I was beginning to understand that I was lucky to have Lilly to look out for me and I wasn't sure I deserved her love and care. Before daylight, I decided to try harder to get along with Lilly, and I promised myself I would pour out the whiskey that was hidden behind the books in the bookcase in my room and I would get rid of the bottle that was in my locker at school.

2

The following Sunday Lilly and her friend Marianne went to a hairstyle show at a downtown hotel. I decided to surprise Lilly by cleaning the whole apartment while she was gone. I dragged the Hoover from the closet and took a dust cloth and furniture polish into Lilly's room. I seldom went in there and the smell of her perfume and the steady ticking of her alarm clock made me feel like an intruder.

I opened the drapes and saw her bed was made and the room was neat so I knew it wouldn't take long to clean. I quickly dusted the night stand, the lamps, and the dresser, then moved to the desk. As I polished the desk top the dust cloth brushed against a stack of letters and sent them scattering to the floor. I gathered up the envelopes and couldn't help but see the return addresses: Office of Admission, University of California, Berkeley; State Department of Commerce, Sacramento, California; Chamber of Commerce of Berkeley, California.

I was sure the letters had something to do with me and wondered why Lilly hadn't mentioned them. I could see the envelopes had been opened and it would be easy to peek. I knew I shouldn't read them, but it would be hours before Lilly would be home so I could ask her about them. I couldn't wait.

I sat down in Lilly's chintz-covered chair and read the letters. The first letter was from UC Berkeley and was a response to an inquiry about the cost of tuition for students who are residents of California. The second letter gave the requirements for getting a beautician's license in California, and the third letter gave information about setting up a beauty salon business in Berkeley. Was Lilly considering a move to California? Was she thinking we'd both move so I could go to college at UC Berkeley?

I was waiting by the door when Lilly came home. "I saw the letters from California," I said. " What's going on?"

"I've been writing for information to find out if we could afford for you to go to UC if we were residents of California. I didn't want to get your hopes up until I knew I could swing it. I think it will be possible, so now you have to decide if that's truly what you want to do."

"Oh, Lilly, Would you give up your work and move halfway across the country just for me?"

"Look...the thing that will make me happy is to see you succeed and have a good life. I'll do whatever I have to do to help you find your way, Rosie. After all, I am your mother."

Lilly and I were packing boxes, getting ready for the Mayflower van that would pick up our stuff on Thursday.

"I really hate to leave this apartment and I'll miss Indianapolis," Lilly said. "I've lived here longer than I've lived anyplace in my life.

"You'll love California, Lilly," I said. "Miss Laurel says Berkeley is one of the most interesting places in the world to live. I'm so excited about being accepted at the university and living in a dorm with Amy for my roommate."

"You're pretty well set. I'll feel better once I have my California beautician's license and get into a salon. I'll have to build up a clientele and that'll take time. I'm going to miss my customers here. I've seen some of them every week for years."

Lilly closed a box, stood up, rubbed her back, and said, "Do you know what this reminds me of? It reminds me of the last time I helped our family pack, just before I ran away with Tony."

She had a faraway look in her eye as she said, "You were only two years old and so cute. It was hard for me to leave you, but I had to get away from Father. I cried as I packed your little dresses and I almost backed out and didn't do it. It was for the best though. Neither of us would have had much of a life if we had stayed with Father."

"You were really brave, Lilly. And you are brave now to move and start all over...just for me."

Lilly grinned. "I'm doing it because I think it will be good for you, but getting a new start may be good for me too. Who knows what will happen out there? Maybe I'll meet a man and find that happy marriage Kate told me about in my Tarot reading so many years ago."

I turned my back and stepped into the closet so Lilly couldn't see the look of disbelief that must have crossed my face. Lilly was already old...in her thirties...and had probably missed her chance to marry again.

I tossed my snow boots and ice skates into the box for the Salvation Army, then reached into the back of the closet and brought out a weathered box that obviously hadn't been opened for a long time. I lifted the lid, took out a small

For Lilly, on your twelfth birthday from your loving father

Luke 2:41-4

white Bible, opened it, and read the inscription.

I leafed through the pages until I found Luke and quickly read the story of Jesus going to the temple when he was twelve years old. I shook my head and wondered how Father, who studied the Bible and pretended to be a man of God, could have done such a terrible thing to Lilly.

"What's that?" Lilly asked.

I handed the Bible to her.

"My gosh!" she exclaimed, "I haven't seen this in years. Let me see what else is in that box."

She reached into the dusty box and took out a small

red box, carefully opened it, and held up a gold chain with a heart on it.

"This is the first piece of jewelry I ever owned," she said. "Tony gave it to me on Valentine's day before we were married."

She put the necklace back and reached into the big box again.

"Look at this," she said as she held up a light blue dotted-Swiss dress.

"Why did you keep that?" I asked. "It's even too small for me."

"This was my eighth grade graduation dress and I wore it for my wedding too. Mrs. Andrews gave it to me when I babysat with her little girl. Her husband was a dentist and they lived in a big house on the prettiest street in Roundhill. She was the nicest person I knew then and I wanted to grow up to be like her."

Lilly folded the blue dress carefully and put it into one of the boxes we were taking to California. I couldn't believe she was going to take that old dress with her.

Part Three

LILLY'S MOTHER
ONLY WHAT SHE REMEMBERS

It seems dim in here...or is it just my eyes? And the smell...it's like they've sprayed the place with floral perfume. I take a few steps and the toe of my rubber sole shoe catches on the thick carpet. I stumble forward...good thing Ralph is holding my arm. We walk slowly toward the dove gray casket.

My husband would turn over in his grave, as they say, if he knew he's being buried from a funeral home instead of a church. Ralph and Lilly made all the arrangements without asking me. At least they do have Reverend Phillips coming to conduct the service.

I look down at the body. The black suit and white shirt look natural and they even put his eye-glasses on him...but he is so still. He was never still a minute from the first time I laid eyes on him handing out hymnals at the revival meeting in Trenton, until last Wednesday when he lay crumpled on the floor.

Ralph tugs on my arm and we move toward the chairs in the front row. I see Lilly and Rosie in their fancy California clothes. They should have worn black. I touch my hat to make sure it's on straight, then smooth my skirt and sit down in the chair between Lilly and Ralph. Lilly hands me a Kleenex. I hate Kleenex and dig into my pocket-book for my starched white hanky.

The music stops and I hear Reverend Phillips say, "Brothers and Sisters, we are gathered here to remember The Reverend Clifford Page."

Remember Clifford...Yes, I remember the summer he was traveling with Reverend Horatio Gray, the famous evangelist, and came to Trenton to hold a revival meeting in a tent south of town. Weeks ahead of time somebody mailed handbills, printed on red paper, to every house and on the night the meetings began, most everybody went out to the big white tent in Mill's pasture.

I wasn't much interested in religion but it was some place to go on Sunday evening, so Imogene Fuller and I walked out there. It was nice in the country with the goldenrod and black-eyed Susans blooming along the fence rows and the smell of fresh cut alfalfa hay in the air. We ambled along, talking and giggling, like girls do, so we were late getting there.

The sides of the tent were rolled up and we could hear the singing a quarter of a mile away. We slipped in to the back of the tent and sat down, hoping no one would notice us. That's when Clifford walked from the front of the tent to the back to give Imogene and me a hymn book. Just the way he walked, with his back straight and his chin jutting forward, made you know he was somebody special.

Still singing, he opened the book to "Blessed Assurance" and handed it to me. He was small and compact and his wide round eyes and brown hair falling over his broad forehead reminded me of James Cagney. He flashed a Pepsodent smile and a big dimple slashed his cheek. I thought he was the cutest boy I'd ever seen. After the service, Imogene and I stayed to help collect the hymn books and I found out he came from Tennessee and had been traveling with Reverend Gray for about a year, learning how to be a preacher himself.

I went every night to the tent meetings, not to hear Reverend Gray's sermons but for the music and to watch Clifford lead the singing. You could tell he liked being up there in front of all the people, dressed in a white summer suit and black tie, and he could get the crowd to really sing out.

Reverend Gray kept his sermons short and at the end of the service, during the last hymn, he would give the call for sinners to come forward and accept the Lord as their savior. On Friday night of the first week, as the congregation sang, "Softly and Tenderly Jesus Is Calling, Come Home, Come Home," I stood up. I hadn't thought about it ahead of time and didn't mean to do it, but something made me stand up. I felt Imogene's hand on my arm trying to hold me back, but I shrugged it off and walked forward and knelt in front of the altar. Reverend Gray put his hand on my head and prayed for the Holy Spirit to enter my heart and while he prayed, I opened my eyes just enough to see that Clifford was watching me.

After the service everybody shook my hand, congratulating me on being a born again Christian. It seemed strange that I could be born again and still feel like the same person I had always been.

Outside, the sun had gone down and most of the people had drifted away from the tent. Since it was getting dark, Clifford offered to walk back to town with Imogene and me. We took Imogene home first and before Clifford left me in front of my house, he asked if I'd like to go on a picnic with him on Saturday, if he could borrow Reverend Gray's car.

On Saturday I wore my pink sun dress and white sandals. We went to Friend's Creek and sat on the grass and ate pimento cheese sandwiches and drank root beer from brown bottles. While we ate, Clifford told me that as soon as he could, he was planning to get a truck and a tent of his own and travel the revival circuit.

"You can make a good living preaching. You'd be surprised how much money the collection brings in night after night," he said.

After we ate, Clifford told me I had the prettiest hair he had ever seen.

"It's just the color of a shiny copper penny," he said. Then he reached into my hair and pulled out a penny.

"This must be yours," he said, dropping the penny into my hand.

I laughed and he held out both hands to show me they were empty, then reached into my hair and pulled out another penny.

"How'd you do that?"

"It's magic," he said. "I know lots of magic tricks. I could kiss you without even touching you."

"Nobody can kiss without touching."

"Close your eyes and hold very still. I'll show you," he said.

I closed my eyes and while I waited, I could smell wintergreen shaving lotion and feel his warm breath against my cheek. Then I felt his lips brush mine.

"Oops, it didn't work," he said, laughing from deep in his throat. Then he leaned forward and I felt his lips full on my mouth. His kiss made me feel romantic and I closed my eyes and put my arms around him...just like in the movies. We kissed again and again.

After awhile he said, "Bet you didn't know you can work magic too." He took my hand and placed it on his crotch. "See what you've done to me...just like magic."

I had never touched a man before and my face burned red. Laughing softly, he stood up and took both my hands in his and pulled me to my feet. He put his arm around my waist and we walked toward the car. I thought we must be leaving but he opened the back door and we both got in. It was there...in the back seat of Reverend Gray's model A Ford that I gave myself to Clifford.

The next week I went every night to the tent meetings and every night as Clifford walked home with me, we stopped at the schoolyard where we'd kiss and make love in the shadows under the fire escape. On his last Friday night in Trenton, he asked me if I wanted to come along when he left town the next morning.

I got up early the next day and went out to Mill's pasture to help take down the tent and pack the chairs on the truck. When the truck was loaded Clifford told Reverend Gray that I was coming along to help do the Lord's work. I climbed into the cab with Clifford so we could follow Reverend Gray's car to the next town.

I didn't even tell Mamma goodbye and I've always been sorry for that, because she got sick that winter and died. I never saw her again.

Some folks would think it was mighty strange that I'd go off with somebody I hardly knew. To tell the truth if I'd known then how a husband can change a wife, I wouldn't have gone, but I'd been wanting to get away from Trenton. I'd lived in that town all my life and nobody there had shown me any kindness...nobody but Mamma, of course, and Imogene. Imogene was my friend only because we were both outcasts...her because she had a father who spent all his time at the corner tavern instead of working, and me because I didn't have a father that anybody knew about.

I hadn't thought about not having a father until I was in first grade and Miss Sebolt handed out squares of manila paper for us to draw pictures of our families. I drew a picture of Mamma and used a yellow crayon for her hair and a blue crayon for her eyes, then I drew a picture of me looking just like her only smaller. After recess when I studied the pictures Miss Sebolt had hung in a row above the blackboard, I could see my family picture was the only one without a father.

That night I asked Mamma why I didn't have a father. "You have a father. I just can't tell you who it is until you're old enough to keep a secret," she said.

I figured my father must be one of Mamma's boyfriends. She had lots of boyfriends who usually brought me a candy bar when they came to visit. They'd give me the candy and say, "You get on upstairs now."

From my room I could smell their cigarette smoke through the register in the floor and hear them kidding around and laughing. When it got all quiet down there I knew they'd gone into the bedroom.

I wished more than anything in the world that Mamma would have just one boyfriend. I was sure that would make people like us better. Even then I knew the people in Trenton disapproved of Mamma and me.

I guess Mamma thought I was old enough to keep a secret the summer I turned fifteen...because that's when she told me my father was Homer Gardner.

"Homer Gardner...the postmaster, who lives in the big brick house across from the park?" I gasped.

"He's your father," she said. "I should have left you on his doorstep. He and his wife could have taken better care of you, but I just couldn't give you up."

I went to the Post Office that afternoon and stared at my father through the general delivery window, hoping he would recognize me and take me home to his big brick house. But he just frowned and handed the mail to me: a postcard and a red hand bill about the revival meeting that was coming to Trenton.

Reverend Phillips clears his throat and reaches for the water tumbler that sits on the corner of the lectern. I realize he's been talking for some time, but I don't know what he said. My mind was in the past.

Determined to pay attention, I straighten my back and focus my eyes on Reverend Phillips. I hear him say, "Clifford Page answered God's call when he was just a young man."

Clifford as a young man...yes, I remember how he looked sitting beside me in the big truck as he drove slowly out of Trenton and headed toward Maysville. I was so happy to be leaving Trenton with Clifford. I sat close to the truck window and leaned forward, hoping somebody would see me with him and know that out of all the girls in Trenton, he had chosen me.

Once we were on the main road, Clifford stepped on the gas. The windows were rolled down and the wind rushed inside the cab, cooling my skin and blowing my hair behind my ears. I felt light and free and wished Clifford would drive on forever.

Clifford was quiet and looked straight ahead as he

drove. I could tell he was thinking.

Finally, he turned to me and said, "Dolly isn't a suitable name for a preacher's wife. You'll need to change it. You can choose a name like Dorothy, Dolores, or Doris."

"What?" I gasped. How could he ask me to do that? I'd been Dolly all my life and I liked my name.

"Think about it," he said when he saw the shock written on my face.

I didn't say yes and I didn't say no. I thought about it all morning and finally reasoned that since I'd been born again as a Christian, it would be okay to take a new name. When we stopped at the county courthouse in Maysville to get a marriage license that afternoon, I signed my name D-o-r-o-t-h-y and I've gone by Dorothy Page ever since.

As we left the courthouse, Clifford said, "We can make it to Winchester by four o'clock if we hurry."

When we got to Winchester we parked the truck by the town square and Clifford unpacked his accordion, then started to play and sing. People seemed to come out of the woodwork to listen. He didn't sing religious songs, instead he sang songs like "Good Night Irene, Good Night," "Meet Me in St Louie," and "Daisy, Daisy." When he sang "Daisy, Daisy, give me your answer true..." I wished I'd chosen Daisy for my new name.

Clifford played "The Buggy and the Ford" on his squeeze-box...as he called his accordion. He played the buggy part slow and bumpy and then the Ford part fast and smooth, and everybody laughed and clapped. He did a couple of magic tricks, pulled some colored scarves out of his hand that looked to be empty and found a penny in some girl's hair. After he finished the show, I handed out handbills advertising the time and place of the tent meetings.

I thought traveling with Clifford would be like being in heaven, but I soon found out he was hard to please. He was disappointed that I couldn't play the piano or lead the singing and my voice was not strong enough to read the scripture so it could be heard. He didn't like the way I talked and corrected every little mistake I made. "Don't say ain't," he'd say. "Don't use gosh and darn, they're just substitutes for God and damn."

He told me I couldn't wear my sundress unless I wore a sweater over it, even in August, and when I put on my red shoes, he told me to take them off. "Those shoes make you look like a whore on Saturday night," he said. The next day I threw the red shoes out the side window of the truck.

In October the nights turned chilly and the crowds at the tent meetings were small. As the crowds shrank, the nightly collections shrank too. Clifford and I were sleeping in the tent to save money and our meals were mostly lunch meat and day-old bread that we bought at grocery stores each morning. When the first frost came in early November, Reverend Gray told us he was getting too old for lumpy beds and cold lunches and was ready to find a church where he could settle down. He sold the truck and equipment to Clifford for a hundred dollars.

Clifford was ecstatic to be in charge, but we missed Reverend Gray. It was a struggle for just two of us to get the tent up and down, especially in cold windy weather. When my hands blistered and cracked so I couldn't hold on to the stakes, Clifford yelled at me, "AREN'T YOU GOOD FOR ANYTHING?" He didn't try to hide his temper after Reverend Gray was gone.

I was pregnant and, by December, I was too sick to help Clifford at all. Finally he decided to find a temporary preaching job at a church that would give us a parsonage to live in.

"We'll go on the road again in the spring," he said.

He found a job in Sunrise, Arkansas. I loved the name of that town and thought having a house of our own would make me happy. But Mamma had never taught me to take care of a house or how to cook. Clifford was really angry when I tried to iron his best white shirt and left a brown scorch mark in the shape of the iron on the front of it. He threw one of my biscuits against the wall and said it was hard as a bullet, and when he came home to a house filled with the smell of burnt beans, he kicked the kitchen door and shouted, "YOU'RE GOOD FOR NOTHING! I MIGHT AS WELL TAKE YOU BACK TO TRENTON."

The very next day I went across the street to Minnie Lyon's house to ask for help, even though Clifford had told me it wouldn't be fitting for me to have anything to do with her because her husband ran the bar on Main Street. Minnie told me that I must soak dried beans overnight before cooking them. She showed me how to sift the flour for biscuits, to roll the dough lightly, and to grease the bottom of the pan. From then on my baking powder biscuits turned out fine and Clifford never knew that it was Minnie who taught me.

Minnie's kitchen was painted bright yellow and seemed warm and sunny even on cold, gray days. She always had a pot of hot coffee and a cookie jar full of sugar cookies. Every afternoon, when Clifford was making calls on his church members, I'd go to Minnie's kitchen. She showed me how much starch to put in Clifford's shirts and how to sprinkle the clothes with warm water to dampen them before I ironed. She taught me how to clean and cut up a chicken and how to make egg noodles. To this day I still make cornbread and chess pie the way Minnie showed me.

When Ralph was born I was disappointed that Clifford didn't want to touch him. "It's your job to take care of him 'till he can walk and talk," he said.

Ralph was a colicky baby and kept me up at night. It

was Minnie who came over and rocked him every afternoon so I could have a nap.

I was still nursing Ralph when I found out I was pregnant again. The babies would be just fifteen months apart. My hands were full with one baby...what would I do with two? I didn't even pretend to be happy about it and I broke down and bawled when I told Minnie. Minnie put her arms around me and said, "You'll love this baby once it's born."

What she said was true. Lilly was born in summer and she was a sweet baby...always smiling and easy to take care of. I loved Lilly and Ralph but I didn't want to have any more babies. I went to Minnie to ask advice on how I could keep from getting pregnant again.

"There's only one sure way that I know of," she said. " You have to keep your husband out of your bed."

That turned out to be easier to do than I thought it would be. As I look back, I know that Clifford wasn't attracted to me because I had gained weight and let myself go. It was Minnie who told me she'd heard that Clifford was meeting the choir director after prayer meetings on Wednesday nights. Most wives would have been angry, but to me at that time, it was a big relief. Clifford could have sex and I wouldn't get pregnant.

The choir director was just his first affair and it was because of her that we had to leave Sunrise. After that, we moved every time Clifford's affairs were found out. I still thought I was doing the right thing until that summer Lilly turned thirteen. What happened then would have broken any mother's heart.

I hear people behind me shift in their chairs and I wonder if Reverend Phillips is preaching too long. Clifford always said the eleventh commandment should have been, "Thou shall not preach a long funeral sermon".

Reverend Phillips clears his throat and says, "Clifford Page was willing to go where he was needed to do God's work."

Yes...I remember how we moved from parsonage to parsonage all across the Midwest so Clifford could do God's work. Some were nice places to live, but others had wallpaper peeling and plaster falling, even mice running in and out. By the time I'd get the place fixed up and get rid of the mice, Clifford would be ready to move again. We often moved in a hurry because Clifford didn't know what some husband might do in his rage when he found out Clifford had been fooling around with his wife.

Of all the places we lived, the one I can never forget is Centerville, Oklahoma, where we lived the summer Lilly turned thirteen. I didn't like that place...even before what happened there. The weather was freezing cold in winter and baking hot in summer.

The church in Centerville was small but seemed to have more than its share of headstrong members. There were two groups fighting to have their say about how to run the church, and of course Clifford wanted to run it his way. There were meetings after meetings and even talk of the church splitting into two churches. Night after night Clifford came home angry, not able to understand why the congregation couldn't see things his way. The church was keeping Clifford so busy that he hadn't found a girlfriend, at least not one that I knew about. I've often wondered, if he'd been having an affair that summer, if things might have turned out differently.

I remember it was hot, the day of Lilly's birthday, and I baked her cake and frosted it early that morning. In the afternoon we sat on the porch and then I let Ralph and Lilly play under the hose. They were soaking wet when Clifford came home...cross as a bear, and he scolded me and the children.

I didn't want to heat up the oven so I fixed macaroni and cheese for supper, and I set up the card table on the back porch. By the time we finished eating, it was dark and all you could hear was the constant hum of the cicadas in the back yard.

I brought Lilly's cake to the table and lit the candles. I still have the memory of how pretty she looked...with her eyes shining in the candle light. She opened her present, a dresser set that must have cost over a dollar, and she jumped up and ran around the table and kissed Clifford. I noticed how he pulled her body close and kissed her full on the lips.

I hadn't liked the way Clifford had been paying so much attention to Lilly, teasing her, tickling her, touching her every chance he got. I could tell he had noticed the changes in her body since she started her monthly bleeding a few months before.

After supper Lilly and Ralph went to their rooms. When I finished the dishes I noticed Clifford wasn't in his chair in the living room. I looked out on the porch, then went to the bedroom...but he wasn't there. I stopped in front of Lilly's closed door and I knew, just knew, he was in there with her. My heart seemed to stop. I stood there wringing my hands... not knowing what to do. I have never felt such despair in my life.

I know now I should have screamed and kicked down the door...but all I could think of was how angry Clifford would be if I tried to stop him from doing something he wanted to do. Instead, I went back to the kitchen and got out the mop bucket. I got down on my hands and knees and started scrubbing, my tears mingling with the mop water. I don't know how many times I went over that floor but I was still scrubbing when Clifford walked past the kitchen door and said, "I'm going on to bed now."

The next morning as soon as Clifford left the house, I went into Lilly's room and took her a cup of cocoa. She sat in her bed, doubled over with her chin resting on her knees, tears standing in her eyes. Her face was as white as the bed sheets and her eyes seemed to have lost their shine. Right then I knew that what had happened had hurt Lilly even more than I had thought it would.

My own body felt heavy with sadness and I sat down on the side of her bed. I wanted to help her, to say the right thing but couldn't find the words.

Finally, I said, "You're a grown up woman now."

Lilly let out a wail and fell back onto her pillow, sobbing.

"It won't hurt as much next time," I said.

She sat up abruptly and narrowed her eyes...staring hard at me as though I was the one who had hurt her.

"Lill--ee," I said, reaching toward her, but she moved away quickly, not letting me touch her. That's when I realized that she blamed me as much as Clifford.

Lilly flopped down again and buried her head under her pillow and no matter what I said, she wouldn't talk to me. That's when I got worried. What if Lilly told somebody what had happened? What if she told her teacher, who might report it to the police?

"Lilly," I said. "Listen to me. You mustn't tell anybody about what happened. If the church people found out, Father would lose his job and we wouldn't have money for food. Father might go to jail and you and Ralph would have to go to an orphanage. Promise me you'll keep this a secret."

Although her head was under the pillow, she heard me and understood what I was saying.

"I promise," she said.

Lilly kept her promise. No one in our family ever mentioned what had happened. Even when Lilly got pregnant she still didn't tell.

We left Centerville the next spring and I was glad to leave it behind. We moved to a little town in Missouri called Roundhill. Ralph and Lilly were both in the eighth grade that year because Ralph had been held back.

I could see Lilly had changed. She was quiet and seemed to have lost interest in her school work. The only thing she cared about was her job babysitting with Mrs. Andrews' little girl. I knew she liked being over at Mrs. Andrews' house more than being at home where Clifford was always checking to see where she was and what she was doing.

That spring, I really started to worry because Lilly had missed her period two months in a row. I didn't mention it to Clifford because I wanted to keep the peace until after the eighth grade graduation that Ralph and Lilly had been looking forward to. I'm sure Clifford knew Lilly was going to have a baby and I was thankful that he didn't say anything about it until after the graduation. Lilly wore a pretty blue dress that Mrs. Andrews gave her and Ralph wore the white summer suit that Clifford had outgrown years before.

As soon as we got home from the graduation, Clifford told us to start loading the truck. He was taking Lilly and me to his sister Callie's house to stay until the baby was born. I didn't want to go to Callie's. She was Clifford's youngest sister and she thought Clifford was perfect and that I wasn't good enough for him. I begged Clifford not to take us there, but he had a way of making me do things I didn't want to do, so we packed the truck and went to Callie's.

I hear Reverend Phillips say, "Clifford Page leaves behind a loving family."

I can't help but turn my head and look at Lilly, wondering if she still hates Clifford. I know her life would have been different if he hadn't used her like he did. That's the trouble with rape...it can never be undone.

It was Clifford's fault that Lilly left us. Over the years I've forgiven his affairs with other women, but I've never been able to forgive him for driving Lilly away. I loved her and had tried to be a good mother to her, teaching her to cook and clean and garden. I didn't expect her to run away from me like I ran away from my mother.

I can't say that I blamed Lilly for running away. I remember how sad she was when we were staying at Callie's house waiting for the baby to be born. And when *her time came*, I wished I could have gone through the labor for her... her young body wasn't ready for childbirth. But when that little Rosie was born, she was the sweetest baby and it was hard to understand how something as wonderful as Rosie could have come out of Clifford's mean and selfish act.

Lilly was upset about the birth and didn't want the baby, but she soon came around and loved Rosie as much as any of us did. We were a happy family that first two years when everybody thought I was Rosie's mother and Lilly was her sister. But then, just as we were moving from Linden, Lilly disappeared. We looked and looked for her and couldn't imagine where she was or how she got away. It wasn't 'till much later that we found out she had a boyfriend who helped her run away from us.

It was Rosie and me that missed Lilly the most. Rosie would cry and I knew she wanted Lilly. I thought of Lilly and prayed for her everyday. After awhile I gave all my love to Rosie...until Lilly took her away from us. My stars, how I missed that little girl and I didn't want to give her up, even though I knew it was for the best.

Well, now that Clifford is gone, I have hopes that Lilly and Rosie will be part of my life again.

I hear the people behind me stand up so I stand up too.

Reverend Phillips says, "May the Lord bless you, and keep you until we meet again."

I watch the dove gray casket carried away.

"It was a nice service," I say as I sit down in the rocker.

"Yes, very nice," Lilly says.

I look over at Clifford's big brown chair and remind myself that he won't be sitting there anymore. I wonder how I'll get along without him to buy the groceries and I wonder where I'll live. I know I can't stay here. There'll be a new preacher and his family wanting this parsonage before long. It's not the moving that I mind...I'm used to that...it's just that I've never had to think about where to move before.

I notice Lilly has put the white table cloth on and the table is covered with casseroles, cakes, and pies the church folks have brought.

"Are you ready for something to eat?" Lilly asks.

"I'm not hungry," I say. "But I might just have a piece of Mabel Finch's blackberry pie."

Lilly brings me some pie. She's a pretty one, that Lilly, and she was always Clifford's favorite. She was smarter than Ralph and she had Clifford's good singing voice. It's just a shame the way things worked out...us not seeing her and Rosie for almost fifteen years. Well...Lilly pulled herself up and has done very well. She took care of herself and Rosie and is even putting Rosie through college.

I glance at the corner cabinet Clifford bought for eight dollars when Paul Wiggins sold out. I have to smile, thinking of Clifford coming home from every farm sale with some piece of furniture in the back of the truck. He was a good provider...we never went hungry and always had clothes on our backs. And he was good with the children when they were small...telling them stories and teaching them songs.

Somehow, thinking of those years, when Ralph and Lilly were little ones, makes me choke up. Lilly sees the tears slide down my cheeks and puts her hand on my shoulder. I place my hand over hers and squeeze.

I want to ask her if she has forgiven me for my part in what happened to her, but instead I say, "Have you been able to forgive him, Lilly?"

"No, Momma, a person never forgets or forgives something like that."

"It will do no good for you to stay mad for the rest of your life."

Lilly clears her throat but her voice still sounds hoarse as she says, "Do you think Father ever regretted what he did? It would help if I thought he was sorry."

I look up into Lilly's sad eyes, "I couldn't say...we never spoke of it."

Dr. Taylor stops by my chair and comments that Clifford was much too young to die. Yes, I think...and I'm much too young to be a widow without a cent to my name. Then Archie Boyd, who runs the Dry Goods Store, tells me he'll miss seeing Clifford around town. I'm surprised how many people who aren't in our church have come. Well, we have stayed here longer than in any other town. I even saw the priest from St. Vincent's Church at the funeral home. He and Clifford became friendly when they served on the Inter-faith Council last year.

Most of the people have gone and Lilly comes and takes my plate.

Reverend McKinley from the Methodist Church comes over and takes my hand and says, "Clifford's death is a loss to our community."

"Yes, and it was so sudden," I say.

"It is a shock, but I had a conversation with Clifford that makes me think he knew his heart was failing."

"Oh?"

" Yes, over six months ago he asked me if there would be a possibility of you getting a job at our orphanage in Rus-selville, if anything happened to him."

I open my mouth but am too surprised to speak. I'm surprised that Clifford might have known he didn't have long to live, but even more surprised that he was thinking about me...that he cared about how I would get along with-out him.

Reverend McKinley strokes his beard and says, "Right now there is a child care position open in the toddler group, that's the two and three year olds. You'd be good with the little ones. You would have a room in the staff's quarters right on the orphanage grounds and you'd get your meals as well as a modest pay. There are several widows of Methodist pastors working at the orphanage until they are old enough to be eligible for an old age pension from the government."

I hold my breath...too stunned to answer. I like taking care of children and I could give those motherless children lots of love. I'd be independent and not have to ask Ralph and Lilly for anything.

Reverend McKinley says, "I'll drive you over there next week and then you can decide if you're interested."

I hesitate only a minute, then make up my mind to take that job.

"I'm interested," I say.

Making the decision feels good...more like the old Dolly than like Dorothy, always waiting for Clifford to tell her what to do. I let my breath out slowly but my chest still feels full...as though it might burst with the pride of knowing I'll be able to take care of myself.

"I'll call you next week," Reverend McKinley says and turns to leave.

When the screened door slams behind him, I look toward heaven and say,

"So, you really are up there after all, huh God?"

I get out of my chair. Now that I know what I'm going to do, I'm impatient to get started.

I go to the kitchen to find Lilly and say, "I'm going to take a job at the Methodist Orphanage in Russelville and I'll be moving over there. I think we should clear things out of here as soon as possible. I guess we can donate the furniture to the church and maybe Ralph can take the truck down to Nelson's used car lot and sell it."

Epilogue

ELLEN ANDREWS
SEEING LILLY AGAIN

I was excited about my first book tour. My publisher had arranged for me to fly to San Francisco and read from my novel in four Bay Area bookstores. I bought a navy blue suit for traveling and a red dress with a matching jacket to wear for the readings. Just before leaving the house, I looked at myself in the mirror and wished I had taken time to get a haircut. I had given myself a Toni home permanent that left my hair curly but without much style. It was too late to do anything about it, so I checked to make sure I had my tickets, briefcase, and bag, then went out onto the porch to wait for Evelyn to take me to the airport.

The flight to San Francisco was my first airplane ride. I sat in a window seat and held on tight during take off, then looked down at the Mississippi River and the Arch before the plane climbed above the clouds. The stewardess handed out miniature pillows and some people slept, but I was alert, listening to make sure the engine didn't skip a beat and let the plane fall to earth.

The sky was clear as the plane descended over the Oakland hills, and I could see the blue bay, the white city of San Francisco, and the Golden Gate Bridge that looked orange instead of gold.

I hadn't traveled much on my own, so I was pleased when I got off the plane and found a young woman in the waiting room, holding up a card with my name on it. Her name was Susan and it was her job to look after me for the next three days. She would drive me to my hotel and to the bookstores, making sure I got to my readings on time. As she drove toward the city, I asked if she thought I might have time to get a haircut.

"There's a wonderful hairstylist right in the hotel where you're staying," she said. "I know she's very busy, but I'll call her and see if I can get an appointment for you."

I went to my room and had just hung up my red dress when the phone rang. I was informed that I could get my hair styled if I could be in the beauty salon in thirty minutes. I finished unpacking and took the elevator to the top floor of the hotel where I found the most elegant beauty salon I had ever seen.

The receptionist ushered me into a private room and asked if she could serve me something to drink. As I sat in the white leather swivel chair, surrounded by mirrors, and sipped iced mineral water from a stemmed goblet, I began to worry about how much the haircut would cost. I was used to Sara's shop in Roundhill where the price of a haircut was about four dollars.

I glanced at the framed California Beautician's License hanging on the wall and read the hairstylist's name, Lilly Belcanti. What a pretty name.

Just then the hair stylist came in and stood behind me. Our eyes met in the mirror.

"Lilly Page!"

"Mrs. Andrews!"

"What a surprise! I never expected to find you in San

Francisco," I said.

"I've lived here about two years. What about you and Trudy? Do you still live in Roundhill?"

"Oh yes, I expect I'll be there forever, but I don't live on Charter Street anymore...." Then words caught in my throat as I told her about Tom's brain tumor and how after his death, Trudy and I had to sell the Charter Street house and move back to my mother's old house, the very house where Lilly and her family had lived.

"I'm so sorry about your husband," she said.

"I'm a working woman now," I said. "I teach second grade and write novels on weekends. I started writing to help pay Trudy's college expenses at Northwestern."

Lilly laughed, "It's amazing what mothers will do to help their children get an education. The reason I moved to California was so my daughter Rosie could go to UC Berkeley."

Lilly picked up her scissors and comb and as I watched her in the mirror, I was remembering the day we bought her eighth grade graduation dress. I couldn't help but wonder if her pregnancy had come to term and if Rosie was that child. If this was Rosie's second year at the university, she would be the right age. I was still convinced that Lilly's father had sexually abused her, but I guessed I would never know for sure.

After my hair was cut, Lilly set my hair on brush rollers and while I sat under the dryer, showed me a picture of Rosie and one of her son who lives with his father in Illinois. I dug into my purse for a picture of Trudy. Lilly said she remembered Trudy's curly red hair.

When Lilly finished combing and teasing my hair, I looked in the mirror and saw that I had a magnificent haircut. I felt younger and more attractive, more in style.

When I opened my purse to pay, Lilly said, "No, no.

This is my gift to you."

"Thank you so much."

"I've never forgotten the gift you gave me when I graduated from eight grade...the blue dress. In fact I still have it."

"I remember how nice you looked in that dress," I said.

"Is there any chance you would have time to come to Berkeley to visit us? I'd like for Rosie to meet you. I've told her about you and how much I wanted to grow up to be like you."

"I think I'll be in a bookstore in Berkeley tomorrow night," I said. "Let me check. Yes, it's Cody's on Telegraph Avenue. Do you know it?"

"Of course I do. I'll be there and if Rosie doesn't have to study, she'll come too."

I left the salon and as I went down in the elevator, I caught sight of myself in the mirror and I was smiling. Yes, seeing Lilly and knowing she had made a good life for herself and her daughter had made my day.

Margaret Judge is a California writer and a member of *The Left Coast Writers Literary Salon.* She grew up in a rural community in the Midwest and now lives in the San Francisco Bay Area with her husband.
Time and Time Again is her first novel.